HARDWAY

JUICE

a novella

by Adam Van Winkle

Cowboy Jamboree
good grit lit.

First Edition
ISBN: 9781099009860

www.cowboyjamboreemagazine.com
www.adamvanwinkle.com

This is a work of fiction. All characters are fictional and any resemblance to persons living or deceased is coincidental.

Cover and Interior Design: Steve Townes
Cover Illustration: Steve Townes

Cowboy Jamboree Press
good grit lit.

GENESIS 32: (24) *So Jakob was left alone, and a man wrestled with him till daybreak. (25) When the man saw that he could not overpower him, he touched the socket of Jakob's hip so that his hip was wrenched as he wrestled with the man. (26) Then the man said, "Let me go, for it is daybreak." But Jakob replied, "I will not let you go unless you bless me." (27) The man asked him, "What is your name?" "Jacob," he answered. (28) Then the man said, "Your name will no longer be Jakob, but Israel, because you have struggled with God and with humans and have overcome."*

For my wife and son, my pack. I love y'all so.

Some advanced praise for <u>Hardway Juice</u> and Adam Van Winkle…

*"If hardway juice is what professional wrestlers call getting bloody the good old fashioned way—no faking, no cheating— then Van Winkle's novella is proof that fiction can cut you just as raw as anything pretending to be "real life." At its core, <u>Hardway Juice</u> is the story of grown men acting like boys and boys forced to become men too soon. If there's a writer out there that's distilled this paradox of professional wrestling better than Van Winkle does here, I haven't found one. But here's the thing: this isn't just a cautionary tale about broken down wrestlers, this is the unflinching story of masculinity gutted and turned inside out with all the ugliness, violence, and tenderness laid bare."
-Benjamin Drevlow, editor at <u>BULL Fiction</u> and author of <u>Bend with the Knees</u>*

"'Hardway juice' is wrestling jargon for bleeding in the ring the 'hard way' (not by intentionally cutting yourself to pretend you've been busted open by your rival.) In Adam Van Winkle's novella about fading wrestlers, small town rasslin', and coming of age through hard knocks, everyone bleeds the hard way. Like in a hardcore, falls count anywhere match, the squared circle in the middle of a high school gym, with its loose ropes, dirty canvas, and rusty ring posts, is not the only place where feuds are being settled. Fans of wrestling will immediately know who the tortured Aurelian is and what he's fighting against but they also may see themselves reflected in the struggles of the young Paul as he

finds refuge from bullying and abuse in this fantasy world of babyfaces and heels, or in George, the reluctant villain who carries the weight of his rival and the world on his shoulders. What Robert E. Howard or F.X. Toole did for boxing, Adam Van Winkle does for the fun mirror world of professional wrestling."
—Gonzalo Baeza, author of La Ciudad de los Hoteles Vacios

"Hardway Juice is a cruel love letter to the small-time independent pro wrestling circuit, the down-and-out performers who inhabit it, and the fans who keep it alive. Like a botched wrestling move that hurts more than it's supposed to, this is a novella that never takes the easy way out when it comes to making readers bleed."
—Joey R Poole, author of I Have Always Been Here Before

It's no secret that professional wrestling has an underbelly — an avalanche of documentaries, tell-all books, and podcasts has revealed men and women crippled or even killed by injury, addiction, and living too fast for too long. In Hardway Juice, Adam Van Winkle grapples through the keenest reversal of all: starting with the hardscrabble world of independent wrestling and the kids drawn to love it for lack of anything else to love, and arriving at a brilliant depiction of the escapism, wonder, and rich history that make so many fans indulge in the wrestling world. Ring the bell-- Van Winkle has pinned down the heart of a sub-culture in a story that has plenty to say about life well beyond the ring ropes.

—Mike T. Chin, author of <u>You Might Forget the Sky was ever Blue</u> and <u>Circus Folk</u>

"The first zine I ever made was a wrestling zine, and Adam Van Winkle's novella <u>Hardaway Juice</u> piledrives me back to those glory days, even if it wasn't always so glorious outside the squared circle. In an arena of fast living where grapplers sacrifice everything for moments of fleeting fame, Van Winkle pins the world of sports entertainment down to its roots of real injuries, cheap motels, over-the-hill superstars, and the desperation of needing so badly to believe in something unreal. In the words of the late, great 'Mean' Gene Okerlund, don't you dare miss it."
—Vernon Smith, author of <u>The Green Ghetto</u>

"In Hardway Juice, the stiffest part of professional wrestling isn't the knife edge chops, it's what happens outside the squared circle, and Adam Van Winkle's novella busted me open."
—Josh Olsen, editor at Gimmick Press, author <u>Such a Good Boy</u>

KEY TERMS

Angle	A wrestling plot which may involve only one match or may continue over several matches for some time. The reason behind a feud or a turn.
Baby face	A good guy.
Blade	The practice of cutting oneself or being cut with a part of a razor blade hidden in tights, hair, under the ring or wrist tape in order to produce blood. Usually cut on the hairline or in the upper forehead.
Blind	When a referee has his back turned while the other side is cheating. Usually done by heels in order to gain the advantage in a match.
Blow off	The big money match to settle a feud between two rivals. The tension builds until it needs to be blown off.
Blow up	To become very fatigued or exhausted, during the match.
Booker	The individual responsible for writing the angles, storylines, finishes of match. Also helps in the hiring and firing in a promotion.
Boy(s)	A wrestler. Being one of the boys, just means you're a wrestler.

Bump	A fall or hit to the mat which knocks the person down.
Bury	To push a wrestler not to the top, but to the bottom until they are no longer relevant or a draw anymore.
Card	The series of matches in one location at one time.
Cleans house	When a wrestler(s) eliminates every other man in the ring.
Comp	To be comped means you got a free ticket to a wrestling event.
Curtain jerker	Wrestlers who usually opens the shows up. Bascially the first match on the card.
Dark match	A match performed before the live TV / PPV show. Seen by the live crowd but not by the TV audience.
Draw	To attract fans. The popularity of a wrestler, the ability to bring in fans.
Dud	A particularly bad and totally uninteresting match.
Face	Short for "baby face."
Fall	A referee's count of three with the loser's shoulders on the mat.
Feud	A series of matches between two wrestlers or multiple groups. Many times they will interview and bad mouth the other wrestler(s).
Finish	The event or sequence of events which leads to the ultimate outcome of a match.
Garbage	Matches or promotions that have no wrestling but pure violence. Use of nothing but weapons and violent gimmick matches.

Getting light	To get light on your oponnent means that you try work with your opponent and get as light as you can so he can get you into in a move. i.e. posting your hand on shoulders for a gorilla press, or jumping up into a body slam.
Go home	to end the match
Gorilla position	The area wrestlers wait their turn to come out for their match/run-in/interview. Most all the time it's the area right behind the curtains.
Green	Not good due to inexperience in the ring.
Hardway juice	Real blood produced by means other than blading. Done the hard way.
Heat	Enthusiasm, a positive/negative response from fans.
Heavy	The opposite of getting light. Basically being dead weight and not helping your opponent get you in any type of move.
Heel	A bad guy; rule-breaker.
House	The wrestling audience in the building
House show	A wrestling event that is not televised.
International object	Foreign object, something not allowed in the ring.
Job	A staged loss. A clean job is a staged loss by legal pin fall or submission without resort to illegalities.
Jobber	An un-pushed wrestler who does jobs for pushed wrestlers. Usually a wrestler who is on a long losing streak.

Juice	Blood. Also means steroids
Juicing	Means two things; A wrestler who is be bleeding. It also means a wrestler who is taking steroids.
Kayfabe	Of or related to inside information about the business. To break kayfabe is to break out of your character. It is also used by wrestlers to kayfabe each other, which means to keep quiet on certain things with other people and to not let them know.
Kill	To stop a gimmick or match that is not getting a good response from the crowd.
Mark	A member of the audience, presumed gullible. Basically a wrestling fan who attends all the shows, buys all the merchandise etc.
Mid-carder	A wrestler who wrestles on the under-card but is usually well known.
Over	When a wrestler's gimmick is well liked by the fans or he receives a great amount of heat whether it be cheers or boos. To be over is to get a big response from fans whenever a wrestler comes out.
Paper	Free complimentary tickets, given to fans and friends/family of wrestlers to make the arena look as if it sold out.
Pop	A loud sudden heat from a house as a response to a wrestler's entry or hot move.
Post	To run or be run into the ring post.
Potato	To injure a wrestler by hitting him on the head or causing him to hit his head on something. He is legitimately hurt from the move.

Powder out	To powder out means either you get knocked out of the ring and leave, or you run out of the ring.
Cut a Promo/ Promo	A solo rant or person being interviewed, that tries to put themselves over by charismatically speaking highly of themselves and degrading his opponents.
Push	When a wrestler starts to go on a winning streak and gets title shots. Also gets more interview time and TV time.
Put Over	When a wrestler of higher or equal credibility to the fans, takes a clean loss to another wrestler to give more credibility to the wrestler's bio and career.
Psychology	To tell a story by working over a certain body part, making a series of moves make sense in the ring. Working the crowd at the right momen, and to sell a lot.
Referee position	Most wrestlers use this to start their match. It is the collar and elbow tie up.
Rest hold	When wrestlers need to take a rest during a match, or figure out the next series of moves, or they can't decide what to do next. They will apply some type of boring non-damaging hold. It only serves to stretch out the match and give the wrestlers time to breathe.
Rib	A rib is playing a practical joke on someone else. Many wrestlers do this to each other on the road.
Run-in	Interference by a non-participant in a match.
Save	A run-in to protect a wrestler from being beat up after a match is over.

Screw-job	A match or ending which is not clean due to factors outside the rules of wrestling.
Sell	Means to act hurt and use facial expressions when a move has been applied.
Schmoz	When a brawl breaks out between several wrestlers
Shoot	The real thing. A match where the participants are really attempting to hurt another.
Smark	A smart mark. A guy who thinks he knows everything there is to know about wrestling. Doesn't care much for gimmicks or angles. Like good matches with psychology.
Spot	An sequence/series of moves which makes a particular match distinctive, the climax of a match.
Spot fest	A match with no psychology. Just high impact moves after high impact moves. There is no storytelling during these types of matches.
Squash	A totally passive job where one wrestler completely dominates another.
Stable	Multiple wrestler's united to form a group.
Stiff	A wrestler who cannot maneuver around the ring very swiftly. He doesn't have much flexibility or stamina. To get stiff also means that all your blows and moves are more physical and hurts more.

Stretch	A form of shoot where one wrestler dominates rather than injures the other as a proof of personal superiority. To stretch someone is to get a wrestler in a submission and stiff him by pulling back.
Tap out	To give into a submission maneuver
Turn	Change in orientation from heel to face or vice-versa.
Tweener	A wrestler who is part heel and part face. He isn't classified as a heel or face, he is more in the middle.
Vignette	A teaser for a debuting wrestler or event, usually done cinematically without an interviewer or real purpose.
Work	A deception or fraud, the opposite of a shoot. Also to work the crowd means to get the crowd into.
Worker	Another term for wrestler.
Workrate	The approximate ratio of good wrestling to stamina in a match or in a wrestler's performance.

WRESTLING ON TELEVISION

Grizzly Smith is no anomaly. Cook County Texas is full of drunks whose permanent disposition is scorn and screwed. I wish I could say it was an honor, remarkable, to serve him beer at the Lakeway Beer Barn, the place I worked in high school, but truth is, he was the same as all the watery eyed sad sack Sunday drunks. He was so stooped that his legendary size was diminished, save his big floppy feet and hands. He didn't even have the big beard—it was more wisps of white hair clinging to his hollow cheeks. With his glasses he looked a lot like my stepdad.

Texoma Texas ain't the roughest part of the country, but a hundred and fifty years ago, it was. And the great great great grandsons of the rough men of the past are still there. Back when, women and children were outlawed from running the streets at night it was such rough country. Back then, everything was named after animals and ideals.

Whitesboro over in Grayson County, where Grizzly was technically born, used to be "Wolf Path." Gainesville, the biggest town in Cook County where Grizzly had spent near all of his life, except of course when he was wrestling on the road, was first called "Liberty." Liberty, TX would be about fifteen miles west of Wolf Path, TX, as Gainesville is from Whitesboro today.

They lynched a Whitesboro man, a black man, named Abe Wildner, in the early 1900s, and there was a hard color line drawn between Grayson and Cook counties. Whitesboro outlawed black citizens. Gainesville did not. I grew up in Whitesboro.

Grizzly Smith's name was on the credits that rolled up the screen after WCW Saturday Night when I was a kid. He was "Assistant to Mr. Runnels." That means Dusty Rhodes, real name Virgil Runnels, hired him. Dusty Rhodes was the American Dream, the most popular wrestler from Texas not named von Erich. He'd hired our local Texan legend to work WCW.

16

I'd heard tell of Smith, and his sons, pro wrestler Jake Roberts and Sam Houston, how they were the local wrestling family. I watched tons of wrestling on television. Rented video tapes of old pay per views from the All Star Video. Jake the Snake was one of my all time favorites then. I always wanted Sam Houston to get over more than he did.

When my stepdad's drinking buddies heard I liked wrestling they were sure to note they knew the von Erichs, who were in Denton and Dallas, the big towns an hour away, and then they'd tell of Grizzly Smith and his sons growing up somewhere right around our little home area. My stepdad and his drinking buddies weren't that different from Grizzly Smith when I did meet, and serve, the man. They slurred these things at me with the same watery eyes he had. Sometimes they called me "queer" for liking to watch men wrestle on TV so much. My stepdad worried out loud a time or two that he was "afraid the boy might be gay."

I had a two-TV-rig in my room. Cable splitters are a wonder and when I figured out the mechanics of 'em around age eleven I crawled in the attic space of our brick ranch and split the cable line and run it down the inside of the wall of my room and punched it through so I could watch TV in my room. Mom controlled TV all night and my stepdad only liked Andy Griffith and Perry Mason. I had the little black and white TV from my stepdad's brokedown Chevy GoodTimes conversion van. Before it broke down and faded in the sun it was one of those decked out vans with drapes and swiveling chairs and space kids could run around before childseat laws, and this little TV. My other TV was scavenged from the Methodist Church Rummage Sale I was forced to volunteer at. It was a big wood consoled colored TV I got for ten bucks. I stuck another splitter on the cable end in my room and run both TVs—the little black and white stacked on top of the wood console TV.

Besides escaping my stepdad's drunk buddies and my parents' drunken sniping and fighting, my purpose was wrestling. WWF aired at the same time as WCW on Monday nights and now I could watch 'em both. Loved wrestling. Was hooked. Watched Saturday mornings and nights, Monday nights, Thursday nights, whenever. I didn't wanna miss a second.

I had my own storylines too. Wrestling characters I'd invent, insert into the storyline on TV. Choose sides. Invent finishing moves. Wrestle the pillows in my room. Had a big fat red beanbag chair for my room from the same church rummage sale. That was Yokozuna—sumo wrestler-cum-WWF champion. I bodyslammed him more than Lex Luger and Hulk Hogan combined. I was a glorious and celebrated champion.

Mom taught me to be such a vicious competitor, I'm sure of that. She made me physically tough. Hit me with a backhand, a board, a belt, whatever it took to keep me in line. She assured me, even when I wasn't so sure, that I needed kept in line often. Sometimes she hit extra hard and I really don't think that was all me. Think that's because my stepdad didn't work and drank too much and sat around watching Andy Griffith instead of trying to find work during the day while Mom was working. At least I imagine that's why.

With both TVs on and me tossing the pillows and beanbag around, jumping from the top rope—the bed—and delivering a flying elbow deep into Yokozuna's throat--the noise of my parents fighting, or even just talking in that way, about my stepdad not working and drinking too much and sitting around watching Andy Griffith were not heard in my room. Ric Flair jawing back and forth with Sting on the microphone on WCW's Saturday Night grabbed me. Held me. Took me away. My parents arguing made me feel gnawing inside my stomach.

A pit hit my stomach at school one day too when Jared Peterson's notebook was discovered by some bully boys with a wrestling sketch in it. He'd made a character. He called his wrestler "Firebird." I called myself, in my room arena, "Little Van Vader." Like I was Big Van Vader's son on account my name had "Van" in it too. They mocked Jared Peterson relentlessly. They called "Firebird" when he tried hard at anything, at school or at sports, made fun of him with it. Thank God I didn't make sketches in my notebook. Thank God I'd never let slip my secret wrestling identity, my prowess in the ring I imagined in my room. I couldn't have taken it all the way through school the way Peterson did.

A small circuit came through our little town when I was in eighth grade. I think it was called NCW and I imagine that stood for National Championship Wrestling. Local legend Jake the Snake Roberts was coming home and he was going to fight the One Man Gang in the Whitesboro High School gym. Jake the Snake was way late. We waited an hour after the second to last match was done for Jake and Gang to get going.

When Jake, Grizzly's son, showed up finally, One Man Gang had to practically lay down for Jake to win as booked. Only after I had a few experiences of my own did I realize that what I saw that night was an extremely drunk and coked up man trying to wrestle.

Stopped following wrestling around the time I didn't have to be in my house anymore. Got a car. That was freedom. I could practically live in it and just sleep at home. Then went to college. I was gone.

In gradschool a buddy showed me the glorious rabbitholes that exist in the internet space for behind the scenes info on all my favorite childhood wrestlers and storylines. I was hooked on wrestling again. Mind you, had no desire to watch it again, Monday nights. Don't need two TVs anymore. Just one screen with internet. And that's almost always wireless, no cables nor splitters required. Just comes to me.

I watched all about what became of Jake Roberts this way. Another son of a Texoma, Texas drunk.

Documentaries got made tracking the spiral into drugs and redemption from addiction of Jake the Snake.

Before his recent recoveries Jake was terribly out of shape and an alcoholic. And, in *Beyond the Mat*, we learned the lengths and cause of his addictions as he scuttled for crack and told of his own conception when his father raped the teenage daughter of a lover. "He was born out of love...and I still love him," Grizzly Smith tells the camera in the next shot. I bet my stepdad that looked a little like Grizzly and drank just like him thought he called me a "queer" out of love.

My wife asked when we hit that space where we really loved each other and we could criticize each other how I could read so much about old wrestling and not care about watching it. I mean, think she's glad that I don't, but she was curious. And I thought about that too.

I means it's interesting stuff. Think of your favorite childhood wrestlers and there's a good chance half of 'em are dead. Overdoses. Suicides. Cancer. Wrestlers are cursed, numbers support this. Big Van Vader, Macho Man, Mr. Perfect, Warrior, Rick Rude, Big Boss Man, Bam Bam Bigelow—don't try to find them on the autograph circuit. Andre the Giant. He died young, but that's to be expected. And did you know Samuel Beckett used to give Andre the Giant who was a neighbor to Beckett in France rides to school so he didn't get made fun of on the bus for his size? Wikipedia is a glorious, glorious thing. Yokozuna, by the way, was dead before he was thirty-five of fluid on the lungs.

I think a lot about Jake Roberts. Probably knowing how flawed he is, and, growing up where he did, understanding some of where the voice and mannerisms and emotional vulnerability come from, knowing the kind of man he was raised by, I look to him as someone who had it stacked against him. Like me his parents were divorced. Like me, his dad was an alcoholic, passed on the addiction gene. Like me, he was abused. Like me, he did enough dumb stuff that he might should be dead. Odds are he would be by now. Shockingly, we're still here.

Sometimes I think I may enjoy reading the behind the scenes stuff and watching the docs and clips now more than I enjoyed watching the wrestling on television then. As I've looked back and uncovered all the things of my childhood that were really going on, I find a lot of veils fall away. Like, what you thought was going on, what everyone was supposed to be working toward, that wasn't real. My mom and that stepdad divorced in my early twenties by the way. And this new wrestling hobby is really much the same. Same as growing up in the brick ranch where we all lived so unhappily, I'm fascinated by how it was really going down, the damage it did in the long run, the survivors and the dead.

AV

chapter 1

SNAKE EATS SNAKE

....

WHITESBORO, TX
FALL 1997

SATURDAY (HOUSE SHOW)

Smells are one thing that comes clear to
Aurelian. Stale plastic popcorn, sweat, rubber, painted
pine boards, and floor wax. Aurelian had been here
once before, had played a basketball game here at
Whitesboro High's gym. Aurelian had been born and
raised one town over, Gainesville, and he was a
Gainesville High Leopard forward in '71 or '72. He hit
a few shots in the paint maybe he recalled. Gainesville
won. He quit sometime after that. Junior year. He was
gonna be a pro wrestler.

Aurelian flushed the locker room toilet twenty-
five years later. He was late coming out. He had to
pull himself together. He couldn't tell how long he'd
been asleep on the shitter. A rinkydink house like this
would get hostile quick. Or worse, bored. He was the
greatest nonchampion the Federation had ever seen.
Aurelian stood, put his baggy back in the waistband of
his trunks and tried to get a grip.

He needed to give 'em a show.

***

"Where you think you're headed to?" Paul's stepdad slurred at him across town earlier in the evening.

The accusatory tone made Paul feel stupid and small. His stepdad was drunk, was bored, was gonna mess with him. He told the truth before he thought better of it. "I was gonna go up to the wrestling matches tonight like I asked about earlier in the week," he offered and hoped it would be enough.

"You and the fuckin' wrestling. Shit's fake. You gay? You like watchin' shiny guys huggin' and rubbin' on each other? You little queer." He took another sip of beer from his rocker-recliner. Paul knew it was his son that was the queer. His stepbrother was older, never lived with them. But he'd cornered Paul a few times. Tried to paw at Paul, make Paul paw at him. "Did you ask your mother?" This was a question Paul's stepdad meant to have answered.

Paul's mom was working at the Happy Stop. She took the job up the street since the transmission had gone out in her car and she could walk to work. She could also sneak beer outta there, cut down on the cost of her husband's beer drinking. "Yea, earlier this week." Paul offered. He was still dumbly telling the truth. "It's just at the high school. I can ride my bike like I do when I go to school anyway."

"Don't be a smart little shit. Only thing worse than a queer is a smartass queer."

"I don't have to go." Paul was beat. There was no point when his stepdad was in this mood.

25

"Do what you want. You just need to mind that you need to ask permission. Ask me."

"Can I go to the wrestling matches tonight?"

"Is it gonna cost me anything?"

"No sir, I got the ticket for reading four novels at school in a month," he lied as even seven dollars would be something his stepdad might make a show of.

"Why didn't you say so? Don't get in trouble. Your mama will kill me if you go get in trouble."

"Yes sir." Paul was finally able to move out the door. He wished he'd made it out the door unseen. He wouldn't have to leave with the humiliation. With the sour smell of boozey insults lingering in his brain.

He kicked a dent in the door of the beer fridge that hummed loudly in the back carport as he rolled his bike out of the carport and down the driveway toward the street.

***

Earlier in the day, midafternoon, on the north side of Whitesboro, George sat at the Dairy Queen. This was a newer model cafe style Dairy Queen. One where old men in this little town, George imagined, could sit and drink coffee in the morning like they did at the gas station cafe in his little Louisiana hometown. George had eaten at a thousand Dairy Queens. Most were still stands, car pull-ups. Fifties-style places. No matter the structure, the chili tasted about the same.

George felt a pain shoot through his chest and he stopped eating. He sat back and put his big paw of a right hand over his chest to try and still the turmoil inside it.

He wished he were back home. It wasn't much, but it had been wiped out in the flood. He needed to wrestle a few more months to get another trailer. He was too old and too out of shape for the road, but at least it came with a motel bed.

As he looked out at the few cars moving by he figured the gate tonight wasn't anything that would put him over. He needed twelve thousand for a suitable trailer. If he could hold out for seventeen, he could get the attached porch and larger hallways. Be nice to have the bigger space. He wasn't as heavy as his Federation wrestling days, but he was still a big, big man.

He worried the Snake would still be in bad shape tonight. He'd been deteriorating with each date. They'd worked their finish out plenty before going on the road, but George was having to carry Aurelian through the maneuvers the last few shows. The crowds were starting to notice. They didn't buy George bowing forward into Aurelian's DDT, pushing him back so George fell with Aurelian's armpit and faceplanting on the canvas while Aurelian tried to wallow off his back and get over for the pin. At the last show, Aurelian stood up and raised his arms in victory, halfhearted as it was, before the three count even went down.

He'd just managed to even find the bastard this morning, get him back to the motel, and put his ass in the bed.

George wallowed in his own self-pity, knowing tonight probably wouldn't be any different. Maybe he should go back to the motel. Get Aurelian up after while. Make sure to get food in him, take him out in the sunshine a few hours. But George wasn't no guardian angel. He was barely keeping his own semiretired life together. He couldn't watch over another dying wrestler all the time too.

MONDAY PREVIOUS

Lisa's stomach hit her feet when she saw the poster outside the gym doors. NCW. One night only. The Warrior. Local legend the Snake. Saturday Night! She hoped to God the paper didn't run it. Hoped there weren't radio commercials. Her daddy'd sit and drink beer at the kitchen table and listen to talk radio on low all day. He didn't read much, but he flipped through the paper. He'd want to go. He'd want her to go.

She wanted to curl up and go to sleep and stay that way for a very long time.

***

Aurelian's dad had been born in Whitesboro, and Aurelian Jr. had been born in the next town over,

Gainesville. Funny thing was his daddy had been all over the country, even seen other parts of the world as a professional wrestler, but somehow, Junior was born just a few miles from where Senior had been.

Other wrestling sons had gotten silver spoons. Greg Gagne, son of Vern, had been pushed to the moon. Erik Watts, son of Cowboy Bill Watts got the same. With no talent. Aurelian knew he was talented, but same as the hardscrabble rural landscape he was born to, he got the same hard knocks his dad got. Of course, Vern and Bill had run successful, at least for a time, wrestling promotions. When Aurelian Sr. went in to promoting, he went under.

Junior thought about Senior when he got the booking schedule. Whitesboro High School Gymnasium, Saturday night. When Junior was a kid, Senior played that his wrestling career was all the way real. He wore neck braces and slings around the house. He couldn't get up and play, couldn't take Aurelian Jr. and his sister to the movies, couldn't even wrestle around with them at the house. He was hurt. He needed to rest and recover before his next match. Then his mother and father split and Senior got married again, had another son and another daughter, and both of them were wrestlers too. Aurelian's upbringing was lonely. His sister got kidnapped and killed by her fiancé's exwife when she was just seventeen. Senior went ahead and kept on wrestling, then started his own promotion down in Louisiana. When that went under, he spent up his favors around the country signing on as scout and talent development for this wrestling promotion and that. Never really came back home until Junior was ready to go off on his own.

***

"Gonna go to see the wrestling little queer says." Paul's stepdad was drunk and it wasn't the watery-eyed stare into space beer drunk. It was the narrowed-pupil snake eyes whiskey drunk. When he picked on Paul the most. "Bet you never tried to put a move on that pretty little brunette." He was talking about Lisa.

Paul's cheeks were hot but he just couldn't muster anything to say.

Fact was Lisa had asked him to kiss her. He had felt under her shirt when she placed his hands there. But just that once. When he tried to kiss Lisa the next day she stopped him. And she never asked him to again. Never mentioned it again. Paul felt that she liked it when they had, but she didn't seem to want anymore.

Paul fantasized about it all the time. Masturbated to it regular. But he'd never say any of that to his stepdad. It wouldn't shut him up and it might get Lisa in trouble if that prick told her dad.

"S'what I thought," Paul's stepdad said when Paul made no reply, and left it there.

In his room Paul turns on the TV. It was Monday and that meant wrestling on TV tonight. He could lose himself in some new prime time action.

When he wasn't watching the weekly wrestling shows, he'd cycle through his payperview tapes. He'd bought them for ninety-nine cents a piece from the used rentals bin at All-Star Video Rental when he stayed with his dad the summer before. When he brought them home, Paul bought a used VCR from the church yard sale, the same place he bought his wood-consoled TV the year before. They'd been on constant loop since.

He knew all the matches. All the moves. He'd watch the tapes so much he started to see when the wrestlers talked to each other, working out moves during the match. He could see when wrestlers feigned good combat by rubbing their foreheads against taped fingers, razor blades hidden in the tape. He watched so much he was becoming a master of the craft, he imagined.

Tonight he could maybe wait for his stepdad to pass out and sneak out to the gas station to visit his mom for free food.

She'd give him some anytime she worked. Pizza pockets, burritos, fried potatoes, stuffed jalapeños—she could fry any of 'em up for Paul from the store supply when she worked. Problem was, if his stepdad knew what he was doing, he'd stop Paul. Tell him not to go bothering his mama at work. She had money to make and didn't need to feed Paul's fat ass while she was doing it, he'd say. At least that was his reaction the first time he found out.

Paul knew his mom didn't mind, but he didn't like to push stuff with his stepdad, and if he pushed on this his mom might get in trouble too.

Paul knew he could wait his stepdad out. He never really bothered Paul when Paul stayed in his room watching TV, watching wrestling. Paul's stepdad only worked three days a week at the most, doing part time construction. Days like this when he didn't work, he started drinking in the morning. He'd be passed out by the time the Monday night show was over. Then Paul could ride his bike up the road to the gas station. Visit with his mom a little bit, and bring a couple of pizza pockets back to his room to rewatch Wrestlemania VIII. It'd be a nice little night. Then, on Saturday, he'd get to see the Snake live.

Life was okay when Paul could think like this, just focus on his pleasure, things that made him feel happy like pizza pockets and wrestling, look past all the moments in between.

***

Lisa doesn't want to hate her dad the way she does. She knows there are worse dads for sure. Paul's stepdad was awful—drunk and a bully. Her dad drank too much, but he wasn't one of those mean drunks. Lisa's dad just got more like himself as he drank. More wistful, more braggy, more silly about the things he wished for and would never have.

That was the pathetic part to Lisa. Getting drunk didn't make him any more honest with himself. It just amped him up more. If he could just or this or that, maybe he could get on in coaching here. Maybe they would create a position for him.

Lisa just wanted out. She'd seen the cycle many times with the other poor townie girls—to overcompensate for the fact that they'd never get out of this place they became experts on everyone's drama and the town itself. Like they just couldn't wait to be one of the adults. It was all, Lisa figured, they would achieve.

Looking around at the adults in this town, Lisa couldn't imagine anything worse.

Lisa had steeled herself for years to leave. Since her mother left really.

Poor Paul. Lisa knew how much he liked her. She liked him too. Even let him kiss her some once— just so she'd have the experience. But there was no point to anything like that. She was getting out. Getting out. Leaving home.

Paul would probably be scarred or sad about that. Lisa felt guilty she'd ever let him get so close. But hell, everyone needs a friend, even her. Lisa knew that much to get by.

Nobody was her dad's friend and he was fucking crazy. Rambled at anyone he met. Some were polite, talking to Lisa's dad about town matters or the football team. Most, like Lisa, looked annoyed, tried to get out of the conversation as soon as possible.

He was annoying her again, asking what she knew he'd ask since she'd seen the flyer at school.

"The Snake's gonna be there!" he claimed excitedly. "You know he's from around here?"

"Then he should know better than to come back." It was mean and Lisa knew it and her dad's face showed it.

"Well that's not nice, girl," he managed in his affectionate but hurt way.

"I'm just not that into wrestling, Dad." Lisa went with a reasoned plea and a nicer tone.

"Well that's not true," Lisa's dad protested. "You used to watch it with me all the time."

"Used to," Lisa sighed, "used to."

***

"Where?" George wasn't sure he heard right. The phone line in the Louisiana sticks often made the other end seem like it was under water.

"Whitesboro. North Texas. Nearly to Oklahoma." Dollar Dave Davies tended to speak sharp and to the point. Years of dealing with promotion had made him pretty matter of fact.

"Oh, okay." George had been out of commission because his wife had gotten sick. He'd come off the road to get her to the hospital for treatments. They were staying with her parents, and George didn't want to put further burden on the old folks. He wanted to stay with his wife longer, but he knew he had to get back on the road if they were going to get a new trailer.

"You're still with Aurelian."

George felt a gnaw in his stomach. "You sure? We've been main eventing for a while now. Dontcha want to give someone else a shot?"

"Not in Whitesboro."

"Yea. Okay. I'll be there Friday night. Should be fine if I leave out of here Friday morning."

"Sounds good. See ya George."

"Yea, see—" Dave hung up before George could finish.

chapter 2

EVERYBODY WE KNEW WAS MAIMED

FRIDAY AFTERNOON

Junior was never afraid his dad would be mad that Junior had done it with his wife. He'd be upset that Junior was so weak he couldn't fend her off. What kind of weak twelve-year-old male would let any kind of woman rape him? No, no, no—this shit was going to the grave. Senior couldn't know nothing about this. Junior wanted to cry, but he knew that was being weak too. After the first time, his stepmom kept at it for a couple years.

Junior wouldn't realize until years later the way Senior had acted being hurt at home all the time. He told the kids and his wives he was injured at work. Sold the fights as real. Told them all he was going to the chiropractors, going to get stretched. What he really done was go drink all day. Bars with cheap domestics on draught. Flop houses with under-undercard wrestlers and whores.

Goddamned Aurelian didn't want to grow up to be like his daddy.

He mostly had though and he wasn't such a drunk he didn't know it. He didn't mess with his own kids like his daddy had. He may not be around 'em really, but at least he didn't fuck with his own kids like that.

God she smelled and tasted awful but he got so hard despite that. Another layer of shame. He was a

37

freak that such an ugly and foul tasting vagina made him so wound up.

One time she was on top of him, grinding her hips down, hunting his hard member with every pump, when all the sudden she started slapping Junior. "You're mine to do what I want with. I control you." She said these thing and more as she smacked Junior. Before Junior realized what was happening he quivered and shook and released inside her.

Why did her hitting him like that make him lose control so much quicker, bigger, he'd wondered.

"Goddamned boy, that was nearly a man-sized load. You must like getting smacked around. Like it rough dontcha ya little pervert?" She then kept pumping and grinding until she shook and moaned.

Junior's daddy was so big—six foot eight inches, over three hundred pounds. A big man wrestler named "Grizzly" in the ring he was such a bear. Junior's stepmomma probably didn't get to smack his dad around like that. When Senior was home she barely acknowledged Junior. Soon as Senior was gone on the road she was all over him again.

When the boys bragged at school about maybe fingering a girl, maybe even getting a girl to touch them, Junior was silent. He'd done everything they could describe and more with his stepmom. But she was ugly and made him and he was ashamed. He couldn't brag about that.

Even when Grizzly got drunk and slapped on Junior and said he was a little boy, when shouting back that he'd nailed the old man's wife would've been the only dagger Junior could throw back, Junior kept silent about it. It was his shame and his alone.

Junior thought about this in his motel room. All that shit happened just ten or fifteen miles west down Highway 82, towards Gainesville where Junior went to high school. He got restless.

He decided to go out, see if he could find something to drink, maybe even find something more. He had to get out of his head.

***

LATE FRIDAY NIGHT

Bruiser Brody had once bent a steel chair over George's head about an hour south of here. At the Sportatorium. Then, all the Von Erichs except David were alive and running one of the most successful promotions in the world outta Dallas.

Brody was there in the Tokyo hotel room to flush the drugs when David Von Erich overdosed early that year and died. Brody himself died three years after smashing George with the chair—stabbed in the locker room shower in Puerto Rico by a crazy fucking wrestler and promoter because Bruiser had pissed the guy off.

Kerry Von Erich shot himself in the chest and died about four years ago about forty minutes down the road—between here and Dallas. Fritz Von Erich died just a couple months ago on the same property. He got lucky and lived long enough to die of lung cancer.

George and Aurelian both had wrestled in the Von Erich company. That was where George had shaved and tattooed his head to make him more menacing to the crowd. Aurelian didn't have the snake then. Didin't have the snake now either.

God, George thinks to himself, I used to love this business.

His room phone rang. He hoped it was his wife. He rolled over from his sitting position in the bed and grabbed the phone on the third ring.

"'Lo," he said.

"George, what the hell happened now?" It was the promoter.

"What's that, Dave?" George asked.

"Aurelian's not in his damned room! Where is he?"

"I'm not his fucking babysitter, Dave. I just wrestle the motherfucker."

"Well you're not gonna have anybody to wrestle tonight if you don't track him down."

"Why in the fuck is that my job? You're the one paying his sorry ass."

"Look George, I'm in Dallas. You're there. And if y'all don't put on a match tonight I won't have anything to pay either of you with."

"Now hold on, Dave, you're barely paying anything now."

"George I've told you how tight this thing is. We're relying on that gate show to show. This ain't the big time."

"Well put me in against someone else. Billy Jack still nearby this area? Ain't he from here?"

"He's from Arkansas. Besides, no one's gonna draw a gate there like Aurelian—that's his daddy's hometown. His hometown practically."

"Goddamned," George managed in somewhat of a sigh.

"Well?" Dave persisted as only a carnival director can.

"Okay. Lemme figure something out. Town ain't that damned big. You gonna reimburse the gas I burn driving around looking for his sorry ass?"

"More than happy to, George. Just get his ass."

"Cuz you know you never gave no gas money the one time—"

"I know. I got it though."

"Okay," George said, though he wasn't sure at all where to start.

***

Aurelian had been in a lotta trailers like this around here. A dime a dozen. Maybe that's where he'd start his biography.

He'd been telling himself for years he was gonna write it all down, turn it into a best seller though he'd never taken any practical steps to that end.

"I mean you could write a book now!" Aurelian struggled to remember the man's name who just said this. They are all the same, fans. They looked at you with this eager expression—like you were gonna fill in the mysteries of the universe for 'em.

Aurelian spent many nights with smack heads like these. Cook meth, sell it off for some better shit of your own. That meth was okay a time or two, but it'd run you down real quick if you stayed on it.

Heroin. Cocaine. You get some function there. Some balance.

"Yea I really should," Aurelian said high as a kite to the man whose name he didn't know.

"Leave him alone," Charley Scott said. He was the guy with two first names whose place they were in and Aurelian did remember from many times like this one. Charlie had caught him in the motel hallway after delivering to a customer there. Had Aurelian follow him out here, like old times. All times.

Charley had been around Aurelian enough he wasn't awestruck or a regular fan or anything like that. And, better, he knew when a regular fan would start to bother and badger Aurelian before even Aurelian knew it.

Charley had seen the fits of rage and sadness Aurelian could sink to and avoided it at all costs.

"What?" the man with no name asked.

"Leave his ass alone. He deals with that wrestle shit all day," Charley said, still light in his tone. His wife and little girl were sleeping in the back room. He didn't want Aurelian getting pissed or breaking stuff.

Aurelian was slipping into a nod, but managed a hoarse whisper: "Yea—don't need to bring that wrestling shit home from the office."

***

George plodded down the worn rug hallway of the motel. It was now early morning but still dark.

He wore a quadruple XL t-shirt, though his stomach still rotunded underneath—pushing the front out well past his gym shorts' waistband and exposing the bottom of his belly.

The shift clerk was leaning on the front desk looking through a newspaper laid out before him.

"Good evening, or morning I guess," George said, feeling embarrassed already. Wrestlers aren't geared for everyday encounters.

"'Lo," the clerk said, but offered no help or prompt to keep talking.

"Well—I'm hoping you can help me." George forged ahead as if a question was asked anyhow.

The clerk still did not respond but gave George attention, finally looking up for the newspaper.

"Well, another wrestler—I'm a wrestler and we're wrestling up at the high school gym later on tonight—another wrestler, he's staying here too, only I can't find him in his room."

"Yes." The clerk offered only his second word but new full well the situation. He had already dealt with Dollar Dave Davis on the phone, been pestered to go into Aurelian's room with a master key to find it empty save a half-stuffed gym bag. He'd listened patiently as Dave yelled through the line when he returned to the phone to say the man was not be found.

"Yeeees…okay, did you see him leave or something?" George didn't want to be rude but was growing frustrated as hell.

"No. Though I just came on a couple hours ago. The early evening clerk was manning the desk before me."

"When will the early evening clerk be back?"

"Early evening I'd imagine."

***

chapter 3

HEELS

EARLY SATURDAY MORNING (MATCH DAY)

Paul had his whole gimmick worked out. He was going to grow his hair big and his beard real bushy when the time came. He'd look like Bruiser Brody or Andre the Giant way back in the day. Wear a buckskin vest and big boots. They'd call him *Wild Man Paul*. He'd be an old school heel.

He had to turn his fat into muscle. The coaches at school were always saying he could if he'd hit the weight room. If he didn't he'd have to put on more weight, get real fat, like Haystacks Calhoun or Happy Humphrey or Big Daddy. He could be *Paul the Wall*.

As he watched the Saturday morning wrestling show he worked on his moves. He had a large body pillow on his bed that he used for an opponent. Snap suplex. Big slam. Drop the elbow. Get heat from the crowd. Pull a massive upset.

After wrestling on television was done, Paul thought he'd go for a jog. It was time to get in shape maybe. He thought maybe that's why Lisa hadn't wanted to make out with him again. Because he wasn't skinny like she was. Like most of the other eighth graders were. Paul was one of the chubbier kids. If he got a little skinnier he wouldn't stick out so much in school pictures. Other boys wouldn't be able to make fun of him in the locker room.

And if he did lose the weight, his stepdad wouldn't be able to make fun of him for being fat.

It was still a little muggy outside. Though it was fall, it still hit temperatures in the 80s regularly. Paul was sweaty before he even jogged a block. Worse, he realized wearing boxers under his basketball shorts was a mistake. His chubby thighs were starting to chafe against his nuts. He was going to chap himself if he wasn't careful.

Paul stopped his jog after two blocks. Maybe a good brisk walk would be a good start, and then he'd wear some briefs tomorrow morning and go for another run. Go a little further.

His face was red and he breathed hard.

As his walk approached the fourth block and he thought about turning back, there was a sudden bark and snarl and yelp.

***

George had been used plenty. He'd never really been pushed, but he'd been used. When they needed a big scary guy he wore spikes and leather and showed his tattoos and grimaced real mean. Then he was billed as from the streets of Chicago. When they wanted to make a jive soul white guy, he pretended like he was black and grew his hair out and wore a dashiki. Called himself Akeem and was billed from Africa.

But this, this shit, just plain old George from backwoods Louisiana driving around in a car that burnt too much gas, looking for tonight's main event so he could get a meager payday, this was the worst kind of use.

Wasn't much to Whitesboro, so George thought he might could spot Aurelian's old beater pretty easy if he was around town. The crux of the town was where the two highways crossed at the north end. If it wasn't for those two highways, George figured, they probably wouldn't book in a town this small, even as an independent promotion, even if Aurelian's daddy was born here, and Aurelian born the next county over.

But those two highways meant there was little more here than some towns about the same size in the area. There was a Sonic Drive In, that Dairy Queen, a Subway sandwich place, and three gas stations.

The motel was on the west side of town, out on Highway 82. George drove east on 82 until he came to Highway 377 which ran north and south. The Sonic and Dairy Queen and one of the gas stations is crammed at the intersection of the two highways along with the Holiday Chevrolet car dealership.

George took 377 south so he could go through town. He split off 377 and took Union Street. Union Street worked south to Main Street. George passed some nice looking houses, some dilapidated houses, a couple of grocery stores. He stopped at the town's single stop light, at Union and Main. He looked both ways down Main Street, an old style boulevard with a big grass divider down the middle. A bank, the local newspaper office whose windows had a couple of flyers for tonight's event, a knick-knack shop, and a lot of empty old buildings. He crossed Main when the light turned green and continued south on Union. The nice houses fell away a mile or so past the Methodist church and trailer houses pocked the country side south of the city limits sign.

With no way of knowing if he was on the right track, George thought he'd go on a little more.

A railroad underpass popped up in front of him. The underpass was covered in spray paint graffiti: *Whitesboro Bearcat Pride. Sara + Blake 4ever. SKANK. WALLFLOWERS 4EVER. Bone Thug. Suck dick.* George couldn't possibly read them all as he sailed under the tracks in a second of shadow and to the other side.

He hit the brakes hard half a mile on. There was a shabby green and white trailer a hundred yards or so off the road, cars and equipment and trash stacked all around, the orange and white Chevy pickup Aurelian had been rolling around in parked near the wonky wooden steps of the trailer's little porch.

***

Paul was startled at first, his nerves jumped and his mouth tasted metallic. His fear turned to disgust though when he realized what the dog was doing. In a neighborhood back yard a great big male German Shepard had mounted and was now forcing himself into a little Cocker Spaniel.

He felt nauseous. This was disgusting. Paul wanted to stop it. He should, he thought, run over and give the big German a Shawn Michael's superkick, powerful smack on the chin with his foot. But Paul thought better of it. What did he know of dog sex? It looked like the little dog didn't want it. But maybe that's just the way it was.

The morning air was hot and sticky despite the October date. The persimmon tree and rotten persimmons on the ground in the backyard with the two dogs smelled rotten and foul.

Paul spun around toward home and broke into a jog once more. This time he wouldn't let himself stop, no matter how winded or hot or uncomfortable his chafing chubby thighs got.

He hitched up his jog into a run and was sailing away from Godwin Park, west on Bagin Street. He got shin splints. At Center Street he went north, going down the hill toward the baseball fields at Center Street and Park Place. His lungs ached and burned. He continued south on Park Place until he got to the alleyway that ran parallel to Randy Street and behind his mom and stepdad's brick ranch house a block down.

By the time he hit the limestone gravel driveway of his house he was drenched and could hardly breathe. He bent over, then fell over the rest of the way, gasping in the grass next to the driveway.

***

Lisa's father banged plates loudly in their trailer's kitchenette. He muttered as he did so. He was being a baby, Lisa thought, just because she wouldn't go to a stupid wrestling show with him.

She knew how it would go. He'd try to catch the eye of a high school coach or a football dad in attendance. He'd go to talking all kinds of high school sports stuff, or try to impress them with his knowledge of the fake sport and fake athletes at the matches.

He crashed another breakfast dish into the sink.

She started to feel bad. Shit always happened this way. She was trying to go along, be numb to it all a few more years, and get the hell out of this town and away from everything as soon as she could. She got good grades. The counselors told her she would qualify for scholarships when the time came. She could do it. She could make it out.

Then this guilt about her dad would gnaw at her. She felt bad. Anyone looking from the outside would just see a dad trying to take care of his house and daughter, making them breakfast, washing the dishes, and all he wanted was for her to go and spend a couple hours with him at the high school gym on a Saturday night.

She knew how embarrassing he was. How people didn't like to talk to him because while he drove a school bus he talked so big and bad. About sports. About the town. About life.

Then Lisa would be furious at herself for being embarrassed. What the fuck did she care what people in this town, kids in her school, thought about her? When she left she was never coming back.

She'd tell her dad it was okay to visit, but he never would because he'd never leave this town. She'd keep in touch with Paul. The rest she would forget and they would forget she was ever here.

"Fine!" Lisa shouted in a defiance that her dad couldn't comprehend. Just to show she wasn't embarrassed and didn't care what this town thought, she'd go. She calmed her tone: "I'll go to the dang wrestling show."

***

George debated opening the door. He'd knocked twice and got no answer. He was getting sweaty under his shirt. He tested the knob on the steel door. It was unlocked. God damned, he might get busted for trespassing for all he knew. But he needed that match tonight. He needed Aurelian.

When George went in the trailer he was shocked to see a little girl sitting on the couch with no shirt on. She must have been five or six. She was drinking a Dr. Pepper and watching cartoons on the TV. Her face was dirty and she made George feel like hell.

A man came hurrying down the hall, still putting his jeans on over his underwear with no shirt on. He was jittery, intense.

"Who you, man?!?" Charley Scott wanted to know. "You're a big 'ol hoss," he added.

"Oh, I'm real sorry to barge in, only I'm looking for the guy that drives that orange and white Chevy out there. See, I'm a wrestler—"

"Oh, hell, why didn't you say so! Bet you're looking for Junior!" Charley's demeanor had shifted from defensive to welcoming quick. He had all sorts in his house on any given day. It was the company he kept in the line of work he did.

"Yea," George said, relieved he didn't have to go through the same spiel he'd gone through with the motel clerk. "Is he here?"

"Sure," he's down the hallway there. I walked him down to my daughter's room to get some shut eye. We were up partying pretty hard."

"I bet," George said, hoping his dejection didn't come through once he had. He didn't want this guy getting upset.

"He's down there, second door on the right. I'll get some coffee going. Name's Charley by the way," Charley offered as he went past the little girl and into the kitchen.

"Thanks. George is mine by the way," George said as he went down the unlit hallway.

He opened the second door on the right and sure enough, there was Aurelian, spread out and snoring on a child's bed in a room with stuffed animals and frilly pink curtains.

53

***

Paul wanted the day to go quickly but it was days like this that it wouldn't go fast.

When he got showered up after his jog home his mother was finally up. She'd putter around the house a few hours, drink her coffee, not pay much mind to anything while she read the paper or went and sat on the porch with a book until it was time for her to go in to work.

His stepdad wouldn't be up for another hour or two yet. He tended to stay up real late then snore real loud well into the middle of the morning.

He thought about going down to the baseball field and see if there was enough kids up yet for a game. The last time had sucked though and he hadn't been back since.

"Not sure you should be here, Paul,' Kenny said that day.

"Why not?" Paul stupidly asked. He knew Kenny just wanted to pick on him. He shouldn't have asked.

"Your vagina is just a little too big to be picked to play."

Beautiful. The funny part was that Paul was good, he was one of the better players until Kenny Heartless and his buddies showed up to the ball field. Paul and the other junior high kids were there nearly every day in the summer, and most weekends in the Fall. The other boys were a year ahead and spent most summer days at the public pool, which is where high schoolers who didn't drive yet had territory, supremacy.

That summer Paul and the other junior high kids played ball on the diamond on the west side of the park every day at least twice a day: in the morning until they got so hot they couldn't stand it and before dinner until they got so hungry they couldn't stand it. Sometimes they'd even go back after dinner and play until the cops chased them all back home.

It was 250 feet to dead center, which meant by 7th grade, those that played PARD and Pony League baseball could hit it out, could feel like major leaguers —picking up RBIs by the bunches as ghost runners came around to score, if they were forced to play four on four.

"Look—Paul's bike is rusty'er than shit!" Daniel Boone—his parents really named him that—chortled and laughed as weezy as he talked as he picked up Paul's rusty piece of shit hand-me-down Huffy.

Kenny Heartless piled on: "Well don't be a dick, Danny. You know his daddy ain't worked in a while."

This was only partly true. Again, why Paul felt the need to clarify could only be the sheer stupidity of being young. But Paul corrected the big-eared ring leader: "Actually my stepdad's been outta work. My daddy works on trucks at Peterbilt down in Denton." This was true, but hardly the point as Danny Boone saw it.

He recovered from his chuckle enough to tack on, "Yea, Kenny, don't be a dick. It's his stepdad that sits on their porch drinkin' beer all day." Danny was incredibly fat. He seemed out of breath from the sentence and grunted as he dropped Paul's bike back down into the gravel.

The bike had belonged to Paul's stepdad's nephew who got killed when he was only sixteen because he was breaking into trailer houses by cutting the screen on the little bathroom windows trailer houses have so he could steel 'scripts and other goodies people hide in their trailer home bathrooms.

Paul'd made it his life's work to restore the Huffy, even though it was really too big for him to ride when he first got it. Now time was taking it again, the old rust coming through Paul's flat black spraycan paint finish, the old style banana seat was beaten vinyl, half duct tape by now.

"Well, Paco, things'll pick up," Kenny chimed in, picking up the ball as Danny Boone was clearly too tired to dish out any more insults for a few moments.

They called him "Paco" because of Paul's dark skin. He was a quarter Indian because his dad was half Indian. The boys taunted Paul with Mexican names and by speaking in fake Spanish around him.

"Que siso coma esto peranza, PACO!" is something Paul might hear riding past the high school to the junior high.

When they showed up that day and made fun of not picking Paul, Kenny and Danny wound up on the same team since Kenny elected himself captain with first pick. They booed and hissed when Murphy took Paul. They even booed and hissed and made sucking sounds like the kind you would use to call a calf to feed when Paul hit two homers against them, clearing all runners, real and ghost.

"Don't get too excited, Paco. We got the kid pitching." Crockett was right, they did have a sixth grader from the block, the last pick, pitching. Kenny and Danny were roaming the outfield, looking to steal fly balls and peg runners, as was the custom for throwing out the offense where no infielders besides the pitcher existed.

They took special glee in pegging chunky junior high kids, like Paul.

That day they did not get the chance. Paul hit them all out of the park. The boys took a break to siphon warm hose water from the back porch of the nearest neighborhood house.

When they were walking back toward the ball field a silver Camaro, only a few years used, came pulling around Park Place Road, which veered west off of Center Street and around the ball field. It was Jared Redfield's car. He was a sophomore going into junior year that summer. Paul had gone to the same daycare as Jared years before. When he pulled alongside the pack of boys, the passenger window came down. Amber Savage was smiling at them. She was in Paul's grade—the prettiest girl in the grade—but she dated high schoolers.

Paul heard, later that summer, she was even having sex with Redfield. He wondered how that happened.

"Whatch ya'll boys up to," Amber said, smiling, only talking to big-eared Kenny and fat Danny.

"Bored as fuck-forced to play with the kiddies." Heartless butted into their game when he was bored, but when Amber asked what he and Danny were up to, he acted like he was doing the junior high kids a damned favor.

"Well, we'll be at the pool. You should come too," Amber said, nodding toward Murphy but none of the other junior high boys.

"Let's go." Redfield put the car back in drive and went off up Center Street in the direction of the pool.

"Pool's crowded," Murphy said to Paul as they drove away. He headed back toward the diamond with his glove, apparently not interested in tagging along with Kenny and Danny to the pool, if indeed they were planning to. They were nice to Murphy since he was the coolest of the junior high kids, but at the pool with the high schoolers he'd surely be their target, being the lowest in social standing, being younger and not a pretty girl.

Danny Boone had been strangely quiet for Danny Boon when Amber was inviting him and Kenny. Now he piped up, still out of breath and wheezing even though he'd just been standing there: "I can't go man. Promised my big bro I'd help him take care of some shit around the house in exchange for him getting beer for me, or us, later."

"Well, aren't you a responsible young man," Heartless said, affecting an effeminate lisp for some reason.

Danny laughed at this, for some reason.

"I'm gonna head home, put my suit on, then head over to the pool." Kenny announced as if the remaining junior high boys cared or needed to know his schedule. But of course, it was just a set-up to encourage the boys to find their inner homosexuals in the park: "You fairies stay here and butt fuck."

Paul didn't know why he sensed it, but he got a premonition. Suddenly, he was very concerned for his bike. On cue, Heartless made a bee-line for his shitty bike while Danny Boone waddled up Park Place toward his house.

Kenny didn't say anything as he reached down and pulled Paul's bike up and walked it back toward where the remaining boys grouped by third base. He was almost serene looking. Almost...good looking.

But then he flashed a devilish grin with wolfish teeth under his big bird beak nose and Dumbo ears. "I need to borrow your busted-ass ride if I want to make my appointments on time," Kenny said.

Paul was powerless to stop it. Paul couldn't remember if he said anything at all as Kenny Heartless jumped on his Huffy and pedaled off under the trees and up the hill of Center Street towards Bagin which would cut over east to Godwin Park where the pool was. None of his buddies said anything, that's for sure. Not that Paul blamed them—they were just avoiding the shame of the awkwardness of the moment.

Paul's face burned and his eyes stung with that shame as he walked home.

He bet Kenny Heartless never felt that way because he wouldn't let himself. He was always so damned cocksure.

Paul's bike was on the front lawn the next morning.

"Left your bike out—it'll rust more if you keep that up," his stepdad came in and snapped while Paul was eating toast and butter and eggs he made himself. For once, Paul was glad that his stepdad thought it was Paul that left it out. He wouldn't know how picked on Paul was—Paul figured that would make his stepdad pick on him more.

Paul just said, "Ok," and went out to grab his bike from the dew.

When he propped the bike up and stepped back to assess the damage, he saw the front wheel was bent, sitting to the right side of the front fork. It made the whole bike pull right constantly when he hopped on it to test her out. Heartless bent the hell out of his front rim.

The bike never again would pedal and steer without constant work. It kept trying to go off in its own direction while Paul constantly steered against it.

He didn't think he'd ride up to the ballfield today. He'd stay safe in his room and watch TV until it was time to ride his wobbly bike up to the high school gym tonight. Tonight was wrestling.

chapter 4

THINK OF THE CHILDREN

SATURDAY NIGHT

Shorty'd never seen nothing like this. Usually he just sat in the patrol car drinking beers while the deputy he was with wrote tickets. Shorty was just a volunteer sheriff's deputy.

"He got hopped up on his own goof balls," Joe reported now. "Neighbor lady says he's been cookin' some kinda dope. Says she's been smellin' it for weeks. Even claims to of called and reported it a few times."

"Oh," was all Shorty could manage. Seeing shit in war'd been one thing because it was war. This was just Grayson County, Texas. The blood didn't cause Shorty to get pukey or week or nothing. The bodies didn't stir much either. He'd seen that shit.

It was the story of it that grabbed him. Gave him pause. The son of a bitch'd hacked up his own wife. It was hard to tell what killed him. Looked like he kind of just give out.

"No wounds on him except old sores," Joe continued his assessment out loud. "Maybe his heart popped. Maybe he cooked up some bad dope on purpose and took it."

"Maybe," Shorty agreed. Seemed as good a theory as any.

The shabby green and white trailer house was itself unremarkable except in its filth. It had the sour smell of whiskey and stale Formica and homemade dope. There were Moon Pie and candy bar wrappers next to empty Dr. Pepper bottles on the end tables and

63

countertops. The carpet was long haired, braided yellow and red and orange fibers so it gave a brown sheen. The walls were paneled particle board. The kitchen was linoleum. There were no pictures on the walls, no little decorative touches that wives install. All finishes felt very temporary.

Shorty'd almost rented a trailer like this a few years back before the man at the VFA showed him how to get his veteran's loan for the little lot and clapboard house he'd found for his little family over in Gordonville.

Shorty'd fixed his stare on the wrappers and Dr. Pepper bottles on the kitchen counter.

"Word is," Joe said noting this, "they say these junkies ain't ever hungry for nothin' but sweets. All they can keep down I guess."

"That right?" Shorty said, finally turning from the scene of blood and bodies and wrappers and trailerhouse finishes to the conversation with Joe Clifford. Clifford was a red headed deputy and one of the real good ones as far as Shorty could see.

"What they say anyway," Joe answered.

"Reckon you oughta get a big truck out here, haul in the whole trailer? Or you want me to just start catalogin' it as is?" The gas infection in Shorty's lungs was irritating his chest in the closed up trailer. It was night but still hot as blazes in the Texas fall. The trailerhouse was starting to feel stuffy.

"Ah hell, let's just step outside and radio-in for the coroner and photographer. They'll document her good enough. It's just domestic." Joe Clifford headed out the door and Shorty followed.

By the time they reached the patrol car, Joe had his Marlboro lit. As he reached in on the driver's side for the radio handle, Shorty reached through the open passenger window and opened the small cooler in the middle of the bench seat and took out another bottle of beer. He popped the top on the handcuffs mounted on his belt. The first swallow was good and cold and opened his breathing back up, or made it feel that way anyway. A couple of beat up sedans and a shitty orange truck were parked about.

"Yea, call Tucker. We need the wagon and the camera for pictures." Clifford let his thumb off the button and took another drag of his Marlboro.

"10-4," came the reply from dispatch.

"Thanks, Bobby," Clifford said into the handle then tossed it onto the seat next to the cooler. "Bet they'll take forty-five minutes or more getting' out here," he said with the next exhale of cigarette.

"Can't blame 'em," Shorty offered, now leaning on the hood, looking at the night sky with his beer, "it ain't an emergency anyway. Ain't nobody goin' nowhere leastwise."

"True enough. I could sure use a coffee or something to eat"

"We'll have to hit the Dairy Queen or Sonic when we get back into town," Shorty agreed.

"When do you sleep?"

"What?" Joe Clifford's question caught Shorty offguard.

"Well hell, you work in the shop all day, then you run around with us all night. Usually hit the bar out on the highway or the truck stop diner or both after. I figure that leaves you an hour and a half or so 'fore you gotta get the shop back open."

Shorty was embarrassed at how accurately Joe Clifford'd pegged his day and that that probably meant this had been thought about and discussed. Joe and the other deputies. Joe and his wife. Joe and the truck stop diner waitresses.

"Just don't need much sleep I guess. And hell, I don't come out every night with y'all."

"Most nights anyway. Ain't judgin', was just wonderin' is all. Didn't mean to rile ya, Shorty."

"Well I just don't ever sleep much. Don't know if it's cuz of 'Nam or what. I get stir crazy if I just sit around the house all night."

"Understandable," Joe offered, seeing Shorty was feeling embarrassed. "Like I said, just wonderin'."

"Keep thinkin' I need to buy a wrecker. Or build one. Make me and the shop more money. Quit just ridin' round with y'all and start workin' the wrecks and scenes."

"That'd make sense. If you gonna stay up all night anyway," Joe said, a twinkle in his eye.

"Joe, come back," the radio barked from inside the cruiser.

Joe threw his cigarette down and reached in the cab again. "Yea, still here," he said as he straightened up out of the window with the radio handle in hand again.

"Yea," Bobby buzzed, "just ran address and renter's names on that location. Charley Scott and his old lady. Child Services has record there's a little boy in that house too."

"Shit," Joe Clifford said, not in the radio, just aloud, before clicking the button and replying, "Okay, we'll go back in and see then."

***

Paul pedaled west up the alley, then took the jog around from the alley to Randy Street. Where Randy Street ran by the gas station where his mama worked Paul glanced over and saw her, sure enough, in the big plate glass window behind the cash register. There were no customers in the store and she smoked a cigarette and stared into space.

Paul didn't stop to see his mom.

He turned left where Randy Street met Union Street and headed south. Just before Clinnon's Grocery Store he made a right on Fourth Street. The high school was a couple blocks west on Fourth.

The parking lot outside the gymnasium on the high school campus was the student parking lot during school days. Tonight, it filled to capacity as the townsfolk showed up for the one-night-only show. As they piled out of their cars many wore old t-shirts, from eight or ten years before when the Snake was the big heel in the big leagues. The old shirts were as faded and wrinkled as the wearers.

Most of the crowd were parents and elementary aged children. People Paul didn't really know. He recognized them of course. He saw their cars go by his house, saw them in the gas station when he went to see his mom. Saw them around their little town. But he didn't know them and figured they didn't know of him.

Paul's mom wasn't from this town, and his stepdad was a high school dropout that didn't hardly work. They weren't people other people would know, Paul figured.

Then Paul spied a beat up four door red sedan he did recognize with people he did know. It was Lisa's dad's car. And Lisa was in the passenger seat, though last Paul had spoke to her she said she definitely wasn't coming.

***

Back at the trailer south of the railroad underpass, they found the child in a closet in the back bedroom. It wasn't a boy. It was a little girl. She wasn't wearing a shirt and her body and face were dirty.

"C'mon now, it's okay," Shorty said and waved his big mechanic's hand in a friendly gesture for her to come on out. She did not budge. Shorty smiled and started a conversation: "You know, you're about my boy's age, maybe a little younger. Wonder if y'all go to school together."

The little girl shook her head.

"Likely she ain't in school anywhere," Joe Clifford said behind Shorty.

"Likely," Shorty replied, then turned attention to the girl again. "I bet you're pretty scared. Good thing is though, I got a magic cloth here." Shorty produced his bandana from his back pocket. He carried one every day. Sometimes black, sometimes red, sometimes, as tonight, blue. The girl seemed interested in the bandana and its powers though she still did not speak.

"See, this is my magic cloth, use it when I'm scared. Carried it in a big war. At night when I was scared, I'd put it over my eyes and it'd transport me away from all that bad stuff that was happening around me." Shorty was impressive in how he handled the child.

As he watched, Joe thought how everyone around town liked Shorty. He was kind and funny and easy going. A war hero and now the town mechanic. A good guy. So many of the local boys turned out to be rowdy men, no damned good.

As he talked to the girl, Shorty grew nervous she wouldn't respond. His son never had much to do with him when he was real little. Was only now starting to talk to Shorty some now that he was at the questioning age. "Would you like to try it out? Just roll it up like this," here Shorty paused and rolled the bandana into a straight line of cloth, thicker and about an inch and a half in width. When he was finished, he continued, "then just hold it at both ends and put it over your eyes like this—" Shorty did as he said and held the bandana over his eyes like a mask. "Then just touch your hands behind your head." He pulled his hands together so he held the mask at the back of his head tightly. "See here."

He held it there for just a moment before removing it and handing the rolled bandana to the girl in the closet. "You give her a whirl," he offered.

Joe Clifford watched in something like awe while the little girl took the bandana from Shorty. She did as he had, held the rolled bandana at both ends and put the middle of it over her eyes, then slowly brought her hands together behind her head and joined them to hold the mask in place.

"Now think of something you love. You may feel yourself getting swept up as the mask transports you but that's fine. That's just how it works okay?" The little girl did not respond to Shorty at all, stood silent holding the mask.

Shorty grabbed her up into his big mechanic's arms and shoulders, was careful not to scrape her too closely against the pins and nametag and badge of his volunteer sheriff's uniform shirt as he pressed her face into his chest. Once she was secure, he hustled passed the scene in the living room and out into the Texas night with Joe Clifford following behind, making sure he closed the door to the scene.

***

Paul's stepdad idled by the gas station. His wife was in there. She looked awful. Skinny and worn out. He took another sip of the Bud and returned the can to its nook between his legs on the bench seat.

He was bored as shit. Used to, he could run up and down the drag a couple times and find a party. Now everyone had moved off or had a buncha kids or had jobs. And he had an ugly wife and her wimpy ass kid.

A cooler sat on the bench seat next to him. It slid all the way to the passenger door as he turned left at the stop sign past the gas station. He drove on up Union Street into the small town night.

***

Paul left his wonky bike at the side entrance door to the gym. He hurried over to Lisa and her dad as they pulled into one of the last spaces available and greeted them as they got out.

"Well hello there, Paul!" Lisa's dad, trying to be cordial to his daughter's friend.

"Good evening, sir." Paul offered. He didn't like talking to dads. He didn't have much practice. He saw his dad in the summer. His stepdad was something else.

"What's this *sir* business? You excited for the matches?" Lisa's dad wagered that Paul would be, and that would make Lisa more excited.

"Oh yea, can't wait."

"Oh *yea*," Lisa mocked. Her dad was wounded by this and let it go there. Lisa felt bad again.

They weren't halfway to the gym door though before Lisa's dad spied the assistant baseball coach for the high school and called out, "Hey Coach!" He stopped and began to chat up Coach Hobson, who didn't seem too annoyed, as Paul and Lisa went on in.

***

Inside, the boys' and girls' locker rooms had been divided into the heel and face locker rooms. The heels were in the girls', The faces were in the boys'. George had made sure he at least veered Aurelian into the face locker room. Once that happened it was pretty well out of his hands.

George didn't want to break the rule that heels and faces do not fraternize. Fans had to believe that heels and faces would never want to hang in the locker rooms, or help each other around the back. He just hope one of the boys kept Aurelian upright and watered until their match. He went into the girls' locker room to get ready.

He'd been up since the night before or early in the morning when Dave called, gone out at daylight to find Junior, gotten Junior back to the room to sleep off what he could, gone for some food at the Dairy Queen, gone back to the hotel, practically dressed Junior and put him in the car and drove his ass over to the high school with lousy directions from the early evening shift clerk at the motel.

He was fucking wiped and he hadn't wrestled yet. That shit show still hung over him. Thick.

***

Aurelian had played basketball in this gym in high school when he was a Gainesville Leopard. He'd always been tall for his age, but never as tall as his daddy.

After high school he told his dad he wanted to be a wrestler. Take up the family business. His dad had a snoot full and told Junior he'd never amount to any damned thing.

It hits Junior that since he played in this old building back in the early Seventies, he had been in this locker room too. Maybe on this same shitter. It's remodeled since then no doubt. It wouldn't have had this short haired carpet or them couches out there. At least he couldn't ever remember playing ball at a high school that had a carpeted locker room and couches.

Coach Buzz was their coach then. Junior couldn't remember his real name, only that the boys all called him Buzz on account of his prominent flat top. Junior can't remember why he tried so hard then.

Like if he got a varsity letter, which he did, his daddy and mom would be happy instead of not happy all the time. By then, when Junior was in high school, he'd lived with both off and on. Of course with his dad and stepmom and their two kids and his stepmom's raging and putrid vagina, then some with his mom and her husband. The stepdad wasn't too bad really, but he went and died.

His momma wasn't supposed to be his momma. She was really the daughter of the woman his dad had been dating. One night, when that woman passed out, Junior's dad went on into another room of the house and raped her daughter. That daughter was underaged and turned out to be Junior's mom.

Junior was named after a monster. He took a big snort of the brown powder he'd made off with from Charley's place. Why the fuck had he ever played basketball in high school, or wrestled for that matter, to impress that mother fucker?

He should really write this all in a book. Make a best seller out of it.

Aurelian Smith, Jr. went into another nod.

***

"I need some air," Lisa half-yelled at Paul so he could hear her over the crowd. The matches had been okay so far.

A fake Ultimate Warrior had run out and flattened some dude in silver tights in the opener. A wrestler dressed up like an Indian beat a wrestler dressed up like a cowboy. In another match, the heel manager got involved and created a big shmoz between the two tag teams and a couple of other wrestlers that did a run-in from the locker room.

They'd been waiting now for over forty-five minutes since the last match for the main event. Something was probably going wrong with the lights or something technical like that, Paul figured. He'd been glad not many kids from school were actually here. He didn't see Heartless or Crockett or the older boys that liked to pick on him. He saw a couple of other junior high kids besides him and Lisa. The majority of the crowd were still town folks he recognized but did not know.

"Want to go outside for a minute?" Lisa asked. Her dad was talking to the girls' eighth grade basketball coach. Lisa probably figured he was telling the coach how much he'd tried to get Lisa into sports.

"Yea, sure. We'll hear when the match gets going."

***

Shorty and Joe sat in the patrol car at the Sonic Drive-in.

"Watcha want, Shorty?" Joe was poised to hit the red button to call the cashier inside.

Shorty kept wiping his uniform shirt, like it was covered in something, though they'd stayed clean of the crime scene. "Oh, nothing really I think."

"You okay?" Joe asked.

75

***

"What's this?"

"That's the old pool."

Lisa and Paul looked at the rotten wood that capped the big empty pool by the field house. The field house was between the gymnasium and the football field at the opposite end of the parking lot. They were just walking around slowly.

"This school had a pool?"

"Apparently," Paul said.

"How'd you know about it?"

"The junior high coaches make us run over here from the junior high and lift weights."

"I can't see you lifting weights," Lisa said, but she wasn't teasing and it wasn't mean.

"I don't do it very good," Paul admitted and half smiled.

She leaned in and kissed him. As she did, the crowd roared inside.

The main event was starting.

***

"You know my daddy used to rape my sister? Drove her into the arms of a killer." Junior was slurring and bobbing badly.

"Okay—knock the shit off Snake," George said so as to address Junior by his persona while they were in the ring in front of the crowd. "Just pull it together and get through this fucking match."

"You don't know man! What is was like around here. That fucking road, that highway right out there," Junior was spitting and pointing wildly, "it runs right by that old country plot my daddy lived on. Right where I grew up with that asshole." The crowd could only see and hear the Snake yelling and shouting. They cheered him wildly.

"I don't know what the fuck to do," George told the referee.

"Just get him through it, Gang!" The referee was a wannabe green wrestler that Dollar Dave Davies paid next to nothing. He addressed George by his persona in the ring. He was proud of his kayfabe abilities.

"God damned," George said, and unloaded a closed fist on Junior. He didn't mind that it hit its mark too well, not that Junior could feel anything like this.

"My sister run off with an older man just to get away from that monster. He attacked her the same way he did my mom."

George hit another right hand while Junior ranted and cried. He then backed up to take a bounce off the rope.

"That man my sister run off with had an ex old lady that killed that man and my sister both."

George hit a massive clothes-line off the ropes and Junior took a flat back bump with a big thud.

"But my old man, he got her pregnant three times before she was seventeen." Junior was blubbering now.

The crowd was starting to boo. Why was the face groveling and being battered?

George kept at it and gave a hard stomp. He was sure he'd really smashed Junior's head with his boot. But Junior kept right on going.

"My sister never had a chance, George! Never had a chance!"

"George, they're turning on y'all!" the green referee hollered, breaking kayfabe.

George snapped. He stomped and stomped and stomped.

***

Paul had his eyes closed. He hoped Lisa had hers closed. He hoped they never stopped kissing.

"Well, myyyyyy gawwwwd. He's not a little queer." Paul's stepdad was standing outside his truck, leaning on the fender, in the nearest parking space to the field house and old pool. Lisa and Paul hadn't noticed it was his truck pulling up. "Here I thought you was coming up here to watch half-naked men and you're up here making out with your little girlfriend." He was drunk. Had the mean look.

Paul felt hot and flush and looked down. Lisa grabbed his hand.

"Little girl, you like this fat little boy? You must you letting him kiss on you like that. You let everyone kiss on you like that?"

"Shut up." It was Paul. He was still looking down.

"Excuuuuuse me? You little pussy, you wanna say that again?" Paul's stepdad ambled away from the truck toward the shadow between the field house and the old pool where Lisa and Paul stood.

"I said, 'shut up.' Just shut up and go the hell away." Paul didn't know where it came from. He'd been made fun of by his stepdad before. In front of Lisa even. Maybe it was the kiss. He didn't want it to end. Now it was ruined. Paul was full of something like rage he found.

"I get to talk to you how I want. The day you can whip my ass is the day you can talk to me any way you want." He approached quicker now, though no more coordinated in his drunken walk.

"I don't want to fight you." Paul said, and that was true.

"Won't be a fight."

"Just leave us alone," Lisa offered.

"Well now girl maybe I want to find out what's so special. You like kissing this little fat boy, you'll really like kissing a real man." At the last ten yards or so Paul's stepdad went into a gallup.

Maybe he was going to just try and scare them. Maybe he really did mean to do harm to Lisa.

Whatever he meant he was drunk. And he stumbled when Paul and Lisa dropped hands and parted.

He crashed through the rotten wood that covered the empty pool. A musty smell went up in the air.

Paul and Lisa rushed over to the edge. He was nearly feet up, his head smashed into the bottom of the empty pool. A snake was in the big empty pool, slithering wildly away from the commotion.

Blood ran and formed a large red spot under Paul's stepdad. He wasn't moving at all. Wasn't even breathing.

***

"Just go home already. Work the finish." This ref was green but it was the smartest thing to do at this point. The crowd realized that Junior was in bad shape and everything was a barrage of boos.

George obliged and stopped pounding on Junior and threw him to the outside of the ring. This was the go home spot and he hoped Junior had some damned semblance of what was happening and could cooperate.

George followed through the ropes and hopped off the ring apron onto the floor beside Junior's body. He picked Junior up and slammed his head into the steel ring steps. Junior just let it happen. His face smacked hard. He didn't block it with his hand at all. Blood gushed from his forehead. Hardway juice.

He was supposed to turn and trip George. Slam him on the outside of the ring onto the hard floor. Then drag him up and roll him in. When George came charging at Junior entering from the outside, Junior was going to kick George's big gut and bend him over. Then hit him with the DDT. Finish. Face wins.

Only Junior kept lying there. Bleeding. George was going to have to improvise again.

George picked Junior up and threw his carcass in the ring. He clamored up and crawled through the ropes. He picked Junior up off the canvas, whipped him into the ropes.

When Junior came running back at him George grabbed Junior's hand and pulled it into his own big gut. Junior was stunned a second by the stop in action, but instinct grabbed hold with George bent forward before him. He grabbed George and pulled him down into the big DDT. Massive pop from the crowd after a beat of confused silence at how the tables turned so quickly.

One. Two. Three.

George practically shoved Junior up to standing so the referee could raise his hand while George himself rolled out of the ring under the bottom rope and scampered back to the girls' locker room.

As he went down the stairs and into the locker room under the grand stands of the gym the roar continued.

They'd gotten through the match. He'd done the damned job.

As he sat on the wooden bench in front of his locker it hits him what Junior was mumbling when the ref raised his hand in victory in the middle of the ring.

"They never found her body. They never found my sister's body…"

Epilogue

PAUL WRITES

WWW.JOBBERS.COM
A WRESTLING BLOG

A YEAR IN THE CAREER OF JAKE THE SNAKE ROBERTS– 1992

By
Paul
Posted on March 27, 2019

THIS YEAR'S OPENING ACT FOR WRESTLEMANIA 35 IS...JAKE "THE SNAKE" ROBERTS. NO JOKE. WELL, SOME JOKES.

Jake is on the Dirty Details Tour (or DDT...see what he did there), and his standup, stories of the road, kayfabe breaking hybrid one man show culminates this year at the Grandaddy of Them All. True, this opening act is 3 days and 34 miles before and south, but still, it's a success story.

For those lucky fans that attend this year, as you plan your Wrestlemania week and weekend, put the DDT show on the docket and make the detour to Sayreville on Thursday night.

The Resurrection of Jake the Snake is no secret and it's great to see after his DDP boot camping he appears to be staying clean and healthy and enjoying the limelight he deserves as a living wrestling legend. Beyond his podcast and rejuvenated merch and branding push for Jake the Snake, he's crafted his one man show and has been touring the country with it to rave fan reviews—at least the ones posted on *JaketheSnakeRoberts.com* appear to be.

No doubt things are looking up.

Of course things look and feel so good because they were so bad for such a long time. DDP found Jake back home in Gainesville, TX, living in a ratty rental just off Highway 82, a few miles west of the Lakeway Beer Barn (confession time: I grew up a few miles east of Jake in Whitesboro, TX and worked at that beer barn in high school; served Jake, his dad, Grizzly Smith, and his half brother, wrestler Sam Houston, many a cheap twelve pack; they never all came together at once as cute as that father-sons hang out might seem). Jake was terribly out of shape and an alcoholic. And, in Beyond the Mat, we learned the lengths and cause of his addictions as he scuttled for crack and told of his own conception when his father raped the teenage daughter of a lover ("He was born out of love...and I still love him," Grizzly tells us afterwards).

After the countless rehab stints and storied and well-documented demons, it feels honestly shocking that Jake is still with us, that he lived to his Hall of Fame induction and beyond to reap its rewards (sorry Warrior), with the shockingly young average age of death of many of his era's wrestlers.

So, as his Wrestlemania opening act approaches, it feels only appropriate to do some career retrospective on Jake the Snake here at Jobbers. As one of the most popular wrestlers of his or any era, a cultural touchstone that ascends to that level of iconic wrestler even the non-wrestling fans know and reference, his career is damned well documented and told.

I here then turn to that briefest of Jake the Snake stints, one he'd rather forget and derides in interviews about that time, one that might not be watched as much, discussed as much: Jake's 1992 WCW run.

It culminated in the astoundingly disappointing 1992 Halloween Havoc Coal Miner's Glove Match (no really, more later) against Sting. While it's not as infamous as the Ultimate Warrior's 1998 Havoc match with Hogan, it's just as wrought with WCW tomfoolery. But we'll get there.

Jake left the WWF after WrestleMania VIII where he Jeff Jarrett-ed Vince McMahon, threatening to no-show the event if not released from his contract. He was pissed he had not been given a position on the WWF writing staff and new a sweet contract offer was waiting where his father worked now at WCW. Ultimately, McMahon agreed, though not before making sure to hold on to merchandising royalties, and Jake showed up to wrestle a fairly nothing match against The Undertaker rather than the blood feud blow off the two former allies should have put on. It is only really noteworthy as #2 on the Taker's streak.

Jake could not wrestle in WCW for 90 days so did not made his debut until August 2, 1992 on WCW's Main Event, where he came out of the crowd to attack Sting and DDT him on a steel chair not once, but twice. When asked by Jim Ross on a televised interview a few days later why he had attacked Sting, Jake responds "Why not?" Well, Jim Ross, wants to know, what if, since he is not a WCW wrestler (kayfabe), Sting decides to press assault charges and Jake is arrested. Jake says he wouldn't be surprised at that since Sting definitely isn't man enough to wrestle him, but "put the right number down for me to sign and I'll sign" Jake assures. He's game to wrestle for WCW and take on the franchise. A few days later, Jesse the Body admiringly interviews Jake where Jake claims he wants the whole world, and Dusty Rhodes and Ron Simmons (then WCW champ) and Sting are just squirrels after a nut.

Let me take a little major swerve here for a moment: Jake comes out of the crowd in street clothes after last being seen on WWF television, attacks Sting and threatens the major organization players in a bid to take over the world, plays free agent not under WCW control and free to attack the promotion, and is threatened with cops and arrest. This is the freaking NWO angle four years before! Pre-Bischoff! Pre-Hall! Think I'm crazy? Explain why Jake, in his first major match (he warmed up in an untelevised bout with Pre-Buff Bagwell in Chicago) at Clash of Champions XX on September 2nd was a Survivor Series rules match where he is teamed with former WWFers, outsiders if you will, Rick Rude and Hercules (as the masked Super Invader). The 1992

WCW creative team was building on the heat of the WWF and WWFers as invaders and heels with similar tactics used in '96.

Okay, back to the interviews. They're telling in many ways.

Jake's comment about the "right number" was fresh on his mind no doubt. His WCW run was soured from the beginning when he got a pay cut before he ever wrested in a WCW ring. He'd received a sweet 3 year, 3.5 million dollar guaranteed deal from future venture capitalist and Turner corporate climber Kip Frey, who stepped down as head of WCW on the 87th day of Jake's 90-day no compete. Cowboy Bill Watts, former wrester and old-schooler took over and put his brand of no mats on the outside concrete and no flying off the top rope on WCW. His brand also involved depriving wrestlers rather than wooing them. Unlike Frey, who offered professional athlete level money, Watts sought to reduce and withhold pay, basing pay on his own moving target assessment performance in the ring. Watts also personally hated Roberts from previous working days, so he quickly tore up Jake's contract and put him on a 1 year, 200,000 dollar performance based deal. No wonder Jake is kayfabing on contracts.

After his pay reduction it does seem Jake's WCW run becomes the "Why not?" he promised.

In the interview with Jesse the Body a few days later Jake drunk mumbles his speech several times, offering a "what I dues" instead of "what I do" at one point, and then loses his line altogether at one point before stopping and looking at Jesse with a smile, then switching back into persona and continuing on. Jake cutting an interview drunk—why not?

The actual matches are about the same. In the Survivor Series match at Clash of Champions XX (WCW insisted on calling it a Four on Four Elimination match, but we can all see) as previously mentioned Jake is with former WWF comrades Rude and Hercules, along with Big Van Vader to take on Sting, the Steiner Brothers and Nikita Koloff. So, Jake and Rude, even though they had an absolute blood feud over the Cheryl tights in WWF—why not? So Hercules as Super Invader, a masked muscular Korean assassin—why not? So Hercules' tights are clearly torn just under the left nipple—why not?

I will say there is a brilliant ending here, and Jake is at the center. It's a standard Survivor Series match where kicks to the back can lead to a pinfall, wrestlers are counted out fast, and any other thing happens to clear wrestlers out of there. After Vader comes off the top rope (eliminating himself from the Survivor Series match because remember this is a DQ in the Watts era) and splashes both the last survivor for the faces, Sting, and his own teammate Rude, the referee is distracted by Rude's companion, pre-Alundra Blaze Madusa. With Rude and Sting out, Jake sneaks into the ring and drags Rude back to the heel corner. He then stands back out on the apron and, when the ref turns around, he slaps the

downed Rude for the legal because-the-ref-saw-it tag. It's an easy DDT and pinfall over Sting after that.
Jim Ross and Jesse the Body send us out of Clash of Champions XX with an exclusive preview of Halloween Havoc 1992, coming October 25th, and it is beautifully bad.

We open with a biker bar and a leather clad little person roaming around with a mustache and a lot of attitude. Madusa is apparently a bar waitress to makes ends meet as she carries around the tray and serves the drinks. Rowdy bikers and the little person give Jake Roberts a welcoming carousal as he comes in. No one is mentioning the giant saw blade in the middle of the room. Madusa continues to serve the fellas and everyone has a good tough time. Then comes Sting. Why these two rivals and foes agree to show up and shoot a promo like this, I can't imagine—but why not? And it's tense and Jake issues the challenge, the "deal": they'll spin the wheel to decide what kind of match to have to settle their score. Jake warns there's all kinds of matches on the wheel, including a "First Blood Match" and a "Death Match" (where, presumably the first wrestler to die loses— why not?). Sting's not scared and he takes the deal. They stand face to face, chest to chest, in front of the buzzsaw blade wheel and…they're eyes turn green and they shoot lasers at each other and they explode! So the wrestlers have exploded and died but they're gonna face off next month at Havoc—why not?

You'd think with as fired up as Sting is in said promo, he'd be jacked to come out to spin the wheel at Havoc '92.

Instead, he comes out without speaking though Schiavone is there, mic in hand. He pulls a lever in front of the wheel rather than spin it. The wheel spins a steady speed before suddenly and suspiciously stopping on "Coal Miner's Glove Match." Sting again says nothing and walks to the back. So your most popular star is NOT going to cut a promo ahead of the match or react to the match decided on by the wheel—why not? And the wheel is clearly rigged—why not? And the least interesting looking match on a wheel with blood and death and barbwire is what they rigged it to —why not?

And the wheel wasn't rigged for the reasons you'd think. You'd think it was so the wrestlers could know the type of match it would be and work it out well in advance so it was as crisp as possible. But not at all. Turner executives did not like blood on TV, so the WCW's hands were well tied on letting the wheel land on nearly any of the other options.

Still, the option they dreamed up is pretty crap. A large leather glove with steel plates duct taped to the the knuckles sits atop a pole attached at one ring corner. The first wrester who can get it, gets to use it. It's a nightstick on a pole match without the backstory of Nailz stealing the nightstick from Boss Man. It plays to nothing in either character or the event. It's just an idea that stuck on a wall apparently. And why not? Watts had no interest in pushing Jake or letting him get popular enough to renegotiate.

90

The match itself before the ending is as blah as the idea. The ending is only redeeming in its absurdity.

As I said, it's not nearly as bad as Warrior-Hogan '98, but it's not great. It's worth noting that unlike Warrior-Hogan which did not close the show in '98 because neither was champ, this one does. Unlike Goldberg in '98, Ron Simmons had to settle for successfully defending the WCW belt against Cactus Jack two matches down the card.

As Jake enters Jim Ross assures us that WCW researchers have developed a Cobra anti-venom in case Jake has his snake with him. Sure, why not? Again though, I must say, WCW creative is tapping into WWF storyline. Though Jake was most known for the boa constrictor Damien whom he most often carried to the WWF ring, WCW focuses on the cobra, his hottest WWF angle when he had the cobra bite Macho Man Randy Savage and slapped Ms. Elizabeth.

The first thing you might notice when you rewatch on the Network is that Jake's belly is about twice as big as it was a month and half before at the Clash. He moves slow, he plays little to the crowd. He wrestles like a man who just took an 80 percent pay cut. Why not? They weren't going to push him. Sting tries, but he doesn't deliver anything more exciting than a flying one-handed bulldog.

The match picks up when Jake gets the upper hand and Cactus Jack runs from the back with a familiar little black bag. He gives it to Jake who starts to dig around in it while

Sting recovers in the ring behind him. Jake pulls out the sickliest black cobra you'll ever see and goes to hold it up to the crowd. At this moment, Sting dropkicks Jake in the back and Jake and the cobra collapsed to the mat, the cobra managing to latch on to Jake's face in the process (because he clearly places it there—why not?). After Sting's quick pin we get an over the shoulder camera shot of the prone and splayed Jake who at this point visibly detaches the snake from his face, looks at it as if something is wrong, then uses the freaking snake fangs to blade (!) before "reattaching" the snake by holding its head again to his cheek. How can we juice on camera if Turner execs won't let us? Let's use a live freaking snake's fangs to blade—why not?

Cactus helps Jake stumble to the back who sells snake poisoning nearly as well as the bandy-legged Savage had.

What happened next is anyone's guess. He was gone from WCW within the month.
Jake has his version and has told it a few times. He didn't like the pay scale or the way wages were withheld until certain performance standards were met so, he claims, he voluntarily went to rehab knowing WCW and especially Watts would fire him for his addictions. He then claims he used equal opportunity employment laws to sue to get the rest of his owed money from WCW for being wrongfully terminated after seeking rehab. It all sounds clever, but, he says, it's also the reason he never was welcomed back to WCW in the post-Watts years as "Turner doesn't hire people who've sued him."

Thinking back on Jake isn't the only reason to go back and watch the Clash XX or Havoc '92 seventeen years on (both available with your Network subscription of course). At the Clash, you'll get to see Andre the Giant's last televised appearance before he'd die in January of '93. You'll also get to see good ol' JR get bullied by Jesse the Body on the call and Schiavone team up for backstage commentary with Bruno Sammartino (who backhands the WWF big time when he says of WCW, it's the "style of wrestling" he prefers). You'll get to see Shane Douglas get booed as face long before he shot on the NWA. You'll get lots of Steve Austin before he was Stone Cold. If only the Network had the dark matches and you could watch future legends Kevin Nash (as Vinnie Vegas) and Diamond Dallas Page have to job to Erik Watts (yes, son of Bill) and Van Hammer before Havoc '92, you'd have a real hidden gem.

I think a lot about Jake Roberts. Probably knowing how flawed he is, and, growing up where he did, understanding some of where the voice and mannerisms and emotional vulnerability come from, I look to him as someone who seemed he was headed for tragedy only to get a hook to grab on to and a turn around in time. I think we'd all like to imagine no matter how much we messed up, that could happen for us to.

I don't think a lot on Jake's 1992 WCW run. There's not enough of it for one. Between the 90 day noncompete and the chopping block of Bill Watts' reign at WCW, it just didn't amount to much. It's a damned shame it didn't. To think that Jake didn't have to be gone from our TV for so long. That he might have tried harder, been in better shape if he was paid and pushed as one of the top star can only be speculated. But it gnaws at me. Jake could have been a major heel and Vader wouldn't have had to shoulder all that load in '93. Jake could have been there to greet Hogan with a DDT in '94. In my perfect world imagination, Jake would have had a glorious run in WCW from '92 to '96, saw WCW into its Nitro years, and then, jumped back to WWF with the same born again gimmick in '96 because he still had to put fellow Texas Stone Cold Steve Austin over at King of the Ring and give him the angle for that Austin 3:16 business. And he would have had a gloriously long second run too.

I wonder if Jake will have anymore to say about his WCW days at his Dirty Details Tour show in Jersey a few days ahead of Wrestlemania. If he doesn't, don't forget, there's a Q&A at the end of the show and you can always ask.

WHY DUSTN RHODES IS AN ICON

By
Paul
Posted on April 25, 2019

THINK ABOUT THIS: IF YOU ARE A FAN MY AGE, 35, THAT STARTED WATCHING WHEN MOST KIDS START WATCHING WRESTLING, 8 OR 9 YEARS OLD, ONE WRESTLER HAS SPANNED YOUR AND MY FANDOM.

I don't want to start a technical debate: other wrestlers have wrestled those near 30 years, but none of those, not Scott Steiner (ten years in Independent wrestling), not Jerry Lawler (gimmick returns, not full time), did it consistently for one of the top two brands on cable. Dustin Rhodes has been with either WCW, WWF/E, or Impact (TNA) when each promotion held such distinction for the majority of that time. Unlike Steiner, Rhodes never really spent more than a year in Independent stints between the big companies.

Alright, I know, now I'm creating the rules for greatness around the man I want to push. But hey, that's wrestling.

And yes, I agree before you object: being in a big promotion does not equal to being the best wrestler. Let Dave Meltzer tell you about Kenny Omega...

So why do I feel so attached to Dustin Rhodes? Why, in the face of AEW's epic announcement this past weekend that Cody Rhodes' opponent at Double or Nothing will be his big half-brother, do I feel an obligation here at TWM to shout out the under-appreciated greatness of Dustin Rhodes?

Because this: more than his endurance throughout my fandom, as the single touchstone I can see now to take me to my first days watching wrestling about 1990, his character and in-ring performance has evolved with, even push directly, my evolution as a fan.

When I was a fresh faced, baby fan of wrestling, there was the fresh babyface Dustin Rhodes as "The Natural" on WCW Saturday Nights, the first weekly show I loved. He wore cowboy boots and was from Texas, just like me. I gathered his dad was the big fat blonde guy on the broadcast team that sounded like my stepdad with that Texas slur. Dustin was a little chubby too, also like me. Gawd, me and Dustin had a lot in common.

WCW liked him too. Where his first short run in the WWF (1990-91) was marked only by tagging with his father, and kept strictly below the mid card, Dustin was booked to the moon in WCW, winning Tag Team Gold with former NWA World Champions Ricky Steamboat and Barry Windham. He won his first US Title defeating Steamboat. He won his second in a two out of three match booking against Rick Rude. They were booking Dustin over some real legends. I just knew this dude was gonna be world champion in no time, and outlast his daddy with the title.

But then something changed. I got older certainly, and for some reason, the uber babyfaces didn't quite have the same appeal for me anymore. I wanted a little edge in the wrestlers I liked, the ones I wanted to see on top. Dustin must have felt a similar itch. After losing his US Title to future all-time greatest WWF champion, Steve Austin at Starrcade '93, Rhodes began a long feud with Col. Rob Parker's Studd Stable, namely Bunkhouse Buck, then the Blacktop Bully (formerly Demolition Smash, formerly Repo Man, real name Barry Darsow). These bouts were often booked as "Bunkhouse Brawls" with weapons and wrestlers wearing jeans. This rivalry culminated with the infamous King of the Road match in WCW's first Uncesored pay-per-view in 1995.

The match is infamous for many WCW shenanigans. The gimmick: Rhodes and Bully would battle in a semi-trailer, while a truck hauls them down the highway, the winner determined by the first to ring a bell at the front of the trailer. The trailer itself was a wire mesh cage on a platform with lots of hay. It was not a live match, but instead a taped match the announcers called as if happening live outside the pay per view. Nothing is hooked up to mics so you cannot hear the action nor is there an audience feed to fill that silence. Yes, many awkward silences ensue. The roads of rural Georgia had been blocked for this, but hilariously a church bus emerged and slowed the big rig and wrestlers down quite a bit. Overall, the match is a big nothing because the wrestlers have such problems staying stable while moving on all that hay. At several points either man can reach out or up and ring the bell, but because clearly it wasn't booked that way, they choose to abandon the opportunity to attack the other opponent like someone realizing they climbed the ladder too fast in a ladder match.

Apparently, Rhodes and BTB had worked out a match sequence where each bladed. There is blood in the match, though not a gratuitous amount by any stretch. WCW decided to edit the match (depsite saying it was live, and that Uncensored was billed as Unsanctioned so this is a big kayfabe breaker) and big jump cuts ruin the end of the match. Eric Bischoff fired Rhodes and Darsow the next day for violating the strict "no-blood" policy WCW mandated at the time (though ridiculous giving the history of WCW and its prevalent blading in the 80s and early 90s).

Strange that Hulk Hogan had bladed two weeks before at a live event against Vader and faced 0 repercussions from best buddy Eric Bischoff. Strange that Bischoff had also been given a "cut half a mil in budget or else" ultimatum from Turner Executives around this time and the firing of Rhodes and Darsow along with Paul Roma and manager Harley Race equalled exactly that. It all stinks of Bischoff trimming budget to keep Hogan and Hogan's buddies paid.

More importantly the feud and the blading began to suggest the dark turn Rhodes was waiting to take with his wrestling persona...

I had two garage sale TVs in my room growing up, one stacked on top of the other, with a cable splitter, so I could watch both Monday Nitro and Monday Night Raw without flipping back and forth. I literally didn't want to miss a minute. Of course, the really cool offshoot of this: I could literally watch wrestlers move from one TV to the other. The top TV was for WCW, the bottom for WWF. I expected Luger on the bottom TV in '95 and suddenly he was the top, back in WCW. I watched as Scott Hall and Kevin Nash and 123Kid jumped from the bottom TV to the top in 1996. I watched Rick Rude do the same on one night in November '97, with mustache on the bottom TV, sans mustache on the top TV.

But Dustin's dismissal from WCW in '95 was a few months before Nitro ever kicked off, pre-Monday Night Wars. As a youngster I assumed one day he would be back on the Nitro TV at some point. I was not primed for him to show up on the bottom TV for WWF, and I damn sure wasn't ready for the way he showed up.
Goldust appeared on the WWF TV in August 1995, a month before the first Nitro. I was not a fan. I didn't like it.

Let's be clear: Goldust is the most ahead-of-his-time, radical wrestling character ever conceived. I was twelve in '95 and still very insecure with the idea of homosexuality owing to

an upbringing in a fairly conservative Christian place.
Goldust therefore made me uncomfortable. I didn't like the
veiled innuendo. I didn't like the lurid touching in the ring.
It all made me...nervous.

Gay and sexually ambiguous characters are not original to
Goldust. Adrian Adonis portrayed a crossdresser in the 80s.
But Goldust's portrayal was serious, not comic fodder
(though yes it's been taken there many times). That was
something very different. For this seriously ambiguous and
menacing portrayal alone, Dustin Rhodes could be called one
of the most impactful wrestlers culturally in the last quarter
century.

But my gawd the move set was still there too. Still patented
Dustin Rhodes (and far more entertaining than anything
Dusty could ever pull off wrestling wise). The skin tight full
body spandex accentuated his uniquely long physique, the
gloves heightened the intensity of his chops and slaps. WWE
put the Intercontinental Belt on him in early '96 when he
beat Razor Ramon at the Royal Rumble, and he beat big
timers to keep it, including the Ultimate Warrior (In Your
House 7, April 1996). I thought then that Rhodes might be
WWE champion soon.

WWE was not ready to put the belt on Goldust though, and
looking back, I can see that wouldn't really have been
popular, especially on the southern swing of the tour in
America in 1996. Instead, the character crumbled a bit in
the years after his Intercontinental run, with the only real

*payoffs to his storylines being shock and scandal (see the
Artist formerly known as Goldust managed by Luna
Vachon). The most innovative turn came with Dustin
breaking kayfabe and playing a born again Christian that
spoke out against the lascivious nature of the Goldust
character (this flexibility has been transgressed a few times
in storyline since and then implemented with the Cody
Rhodes Stardust character). By the time Dustin was
decrying Goldust, I had finally accepted him, cheered for
him. Maybe this was even because Dustin decried it—I was
an angsty teen by then and squarely left of the Christian
right.*

*Unfortunately Rhodes' personal life, conflicts, and abuses
have derailed him at opportune moments. His marriage to
Teri Runnels (aka Marlena) estranged him from his father
(who stayed with WCW until its 2001 demise), and his
divorce from Teri and subsequent substance abuse estranged
him from the WWF. In 1999, when really Goldust should
have risen to prominence alongside The Rock and HHH,
Dustin headed back to WCW.*

*WCW created a character, Seven, based on the film noir Dark
City, who had a painted white face and stared at children
through their bedroom windows. WCW executives did not
like the child abductor angle and the character was
abandoned with Rhodes doing a worked shoot on Nitro about
how he despised such made up characters and just wanted to
wrestle as himself. Here he took the persona of the
"American Nightmare," a nod to his father of course, and he*

stayed with WCW until it went under, wrestling on the last WCW pay-per-view ever, Greed in March 2001. Ironically, this WCW run ended the way his first WWF run did: tag teaming with his father on a pay-per-view.

When the WWF bought WCW in 2001, they couldn't wait to run vignettes hinting at the return of Goldust, and brought him back officially at the start of 2002 in the Royal Rumble. This second Goldust run was marked by his rivalries within the Hardcore division, and his 9 Hardcore titles (remember, that title was often won and lost multiple times on a single day).

In 2002 a new side of Goldust was revealed: he's funny and makes great tag teams. His first teaming was with Booker T. They created some fantastic vignettes and after feuding with the nWo (yes, really in WWF 2002), won the Tag Team Titles. An interesting angle was set up for Goldust and Booker T to feud after their split, though Rhodes's WWE contract was not renewed.

He showed up in the early TNA incarnation and challenged Jeff Jarrett for the NWA world title as "Lone Star" Dustin Rhodes. TNA booked Rhodes very well, having him beat established workers like Raven, as well as up and comers like Bobby Roode and Kid Kash. They booked him so well, when his TNA contract was up in 2005 Rhodes jumped back to WWE.

This run was rather sporadic. Real life Dustin Runnels no-showed some events and was released in 2006. For 2007 and 2008 it was back to TNA.

This run was marked by the appearance of Black Reign, pitched as Dustin Rhodes split personality that had scarred Rhodes since an early age. He was booked primarily against the roster freaks like Abyss and Raven and Rhino in matches called "Monster's Ball" and and "Shop of Horrors" and "Match of 10,000 Tacks." The once remarkable and singular freak Goldust was now just another "bizarre" gimmick for this TNA run.

In 2009 Goldust was back again in the WWE. If you haven't noticed by now, this character had now survived over a decade amid very shifting sands in the industry. He swapped back and forth for WWE brands, between ECW, RAW and NXT (as a pro). This run was highlighted by the Runnels' family reunion. Vince McMahon had for years made a mockery of Dusty Rhodes, real life Virgil Runnels (it's why Ted DiBiase Sr.'s valet was named "Virgil," it's why Dusty had to wear polkadots in his late 80s WWF run). But as with many things in the wake of the rise of the monolith of WWE and its control over most defunct promotions and libraries, the WWE's outlook and promotion of the history of the sport has changed. This 2009-2010 run was really highlighted by the reunion of Dusty and Dustin in storyline, and the introduction of the 3rd Runnels, Cody Rhodes.

Through his long injury in 2011 and 2012 Dustin Rhodes still got TV time as a WWE producer, especially when it came to vignettes ands stories including Dusty and Cody.

Fully recovered and returning to the WWE ring in 2013 at the Royal Rumble, Goldust continued to be put into storylines with Cody, forming a tag team and defeating then champs Seth Rollins and Roman Reigns, until, naturally, they feuded and split in storyline. Cody introduced Stardust and the two teamed once again, winning the Tag Team Championship by defeating the Usos. When Stardust and Goldust eventually split, Goldust got the upper hand in their feud, winning against Stardust at Fastlane in February 2015 and continuing the feud in various storylines through the end of the year.

2016 was marked by the run of the Golden Truth, a tag team of Goldust and R. Truth teased for months to open the year, carrying all the way to May 2017 when Goldust would turn definitively heel for the first time in a while by attacking R. Truth.
After the subsequent rivalry with Truth, Goldust was briefly mingled into the Bray Wyatt and Finn Balor rivalry, with Wyatt wiping Goldust's facepaint away. He reemerged that year to wrestle as "The Natural" Dustin Rhodes once again at Starrcade 2017, 22 years after Goldust was introduced.

By July 2018 Rhodes' knees needed surgery and that is where he has been, recovering, waiting to challenge his brother now at AEW's Double or Nothing.

WHEW! Can you even take all that in? This guy was beating Steamboat and Rude to win titles back in the day, and here he is beating Dash Wilder in 2017. Put it another way: Bray Wyatt is the nephew of the guy Dustin won his second tag team title with in WCW in 1991, Barry Windham. He debuted as Goldust 3 months after 9 year-old Cody was at Slamboree 1995 standing by Dusty as the American Dream was inducted into the WCW Hall of Fame.

Dustin Rhodes/Goldust's staying power in a business that offers little in the way of stability over time is truly remarkable, especially when you consider he's never been the typical wrestling body, and no promotion ever put the big belt on him.
I know part of it this is his family name. The Rhodes must be the second most famous wrestling family from Texas (let's call the Von Erichs number 1 and not debate), and father like oldest son wrestled for decades. But let's be clear, Dustin Rhodes did something wholly on his own with the Goldust gimmick, and made it so valuable his younger brother was storylined into the Stardust gimmick. Dustin, not Dusty, shaped the ultimate WWE fate of the Rhodes.

Dustin Rhodes' match with Cody Rhodes was introduced in a scintillating AEW vignette on April 21st that blended the kayfabe Rhodes and IRL Runnels worlds. I can't wait for this epic matchup, this culmination of a wrestling family saga that spans promotions and generations (a saga I will look to explore in more detail here at TWM in the month before the matchup).

Whatever happens in May with Cody, I know this now: Dustin Rhodes has mattered as much to this fan as anyone in wrestling in the time I've watched…and he's the only one that has been there the whole time.

THE LONG RHODES HOME: A RHODES FAMILY RETROSPECTIVE

By
Paul
Posted on May 3, 2019

TEXAS HAS PRODUCED LEGENDARY WRESTLING FAMILIES.

The Funks. The Von Erichs. The Windhams. The Guerreros. The Smiths (Grizzly Smith, Jake Roberts, Sam Houston). Legacies from these still appear on our screen today—see Bray Wyatt (Windham) and Chavo Guerrero. But none, no other family, has had the lasting impact and staying power on the biggest stages of wrestling as the Rhodes family.

It is no surprise then that Dustin's promo video released to announce the epic brother-brother matchup of Dustin and Cody Rhodes at AEW's Double or Nothing in May focused on family, filmed no doubt on his Texas country spread. Dustin quips therein that Cody's goal is to put Dustin out to pasture at 50. He laments, as Dusty once did in a WCW Clash of Champions promo to align with Dustin against Arn Anderson and Bunkhouse Buck of the Stud Stable, that Cody, the younger brother, was given the privileged upbringing Dustin never had. Cody has more recently responded that the match is bigger than sibling rivalry. It's

Cody's generation versus Dustin's. It's Cody and AEW's attempt to destroy the Attitude Era generation's stronghold on the sport.

"I'm not here to kill Dustin Rhodes. I'm here to kill the Attitude Era," Cody said.
Both have painted a colorful narrative about why this match is going down. This match got heat.

But that shouldn't be a shock either. Look at their father. Look at The Son of a Plumber, The American Dream Dusty Rhodes, master of the colorful turn of phrase, master of the match building rant.

Look no further than his famous "Hard Times" promo ahead of his Starrcade '85 bout with Ric Flair for the world title:

First of all, I would to thank the many, many fans throughout this country that wrote cards and letters to Dusty Rhodes, The American Dream, while I was down. Secondly, I want to thank Jim Crockett promotions for waitin' and takin' the time 'cause I know how important it was, Starrcade '85 it is to the wrestling fans, it is to Jim Crockett promotions, and Dusty Rhodes The American Dream. With that wait, I got what I wanted, Ric Flair the World's Heavyweight Champion. I don't have to say a whole lot more about the way I feel about Ric Flair; no respect, no honor. There is no honor amongst thieves in the first place.

He put hard times on Dusty Rhodes and his family.
You don't know what hard times are daddy. Hard
times are when the textile workers around this country
are out of work, they got 4 or 5 kids and can't pay their
wages, can't buy their food. Hard times are when the
auto workers are out of work and they tell 'em go
home. And hard times are when a man has worked at a
job for thirty years, thirty years, and they give him a
watch, kick him in the butt and say "hey a computer
took your place, daddy", that's hard times! That's hard
times! And Ric Flair you put hard times on this
country by takin' Dusty Rhodes out, that's hard times.
And we all had hard times together, and I admit, I
don't look like the athlete of the day supposed to look.
My belly's just a lil' big, my heiny's a lil' big, but
brother, I am bad. And they know I'm bad.

There were two bad people... One was John Wayne and
he's dead brother, and the other's right here. Nature
Boy Ric Flair, the World's Heavyweight title belongs
to these people. I'mma reach out right now, I want you
at home to know my hand is touchin' your hand for the
gathering of the biggest body of people in this country,
in this universe, all over the world now, reachin' out
because the love that was given me and this time I will
repay you now. Because I will be the next World's
Heavyweight Champion on this hard time blues. Dusty
Rhodes tour, '85.

And Ric Flair, Nature Boy... Let me leave you with this. One way to hurt Ric Flair, is to take what he cherishes more than anything in the world and that's the World's Heavyweight title. I'm gon' take it, I been there twice. This time when I take it daddy, I'm gon' take it for you. Let's gather for it. Don't let me down now, 'cause I came back for you, for that man upstairs that died 10-12 years ago and never got the opportunity to see a real World's Champion. And I'm proud of you, thank god I have you, and I love you. I love you!

See what I mean? Those goosebumps you've got right now are real. It doesn't matter that part of it gets nonsensical (I mean, I hope the textile workers don't have to pay their own wages). In fact, the charm of his erroneous word choice at times comes precisely from a seemingly genuine flustering frustration of the Hard Times with which he identifies himself here against the bourgeois Flair persona.

Starccade '85 was The Son of the Plumber versus The Golden Boy—jet-flying, limo-ridin', kiss-stealin' party boy. No one in the arena or on the pay-per-view audience would have felt it on that level without The American Dream Dusty Rhodes.

Here we are, 34 years later, and the sons of The Son of the Plumber have the stage on the most anticipated non-WWE pay-per-view in years.

Dustin and Cody have done a lot in their respective careers to distinguish themselves from Dusty and each other. I think I can say without question the sons far surpass the in-ring working ability of the father. Both have impacted the wrestling world and driven central storylines through their personas and promo, just like Dusty. In a way that the Funks, Von Erichs, Windhams, Smiths, and Guerreros never achieved, ALL of the wrestling family members have made and stayed in the big time.

Dustin has been a mainstay for 30 years. He started in WCW in '89, then exploded the mold as Goldust off and on for the past 25 years. Cody first appeared at Slamboree '95, a nine year old standing with his famous father as Dusty was inducted into the WCW Legends Hall of Fame. He earned his way into the big time, spending a decade working up the WWE food chain, OVW to NXT to Raw, from 2006-2016. In 2016 he declared independence, and on Dave Meltzer's challenge, has launched AEW with funding from the Khan family.

And Cody is certainly primed to run the show. Dusty Rhodes ran Florida and WCW booking for years as a wrestler/booking agent for both promotions from the 1970s through the 1990s. Look it up and you'll find the "Dusty Finish" is legitimate wrestling lingo for a booking that appears to have one wrestler win only to have the decision quickly reversed on a technicality. Others did it before, but Dusty booked it often. After WCW fell to the WWE monolith in 2001, Dusty started his own promotion, *Turnbuckle Championship Wrestling*, siphoning off WCW backstage and in ring talent among those not picked up by WWE close to the old WCW flagship, Marietta, GA. After Turnbuckle, Dusty moved over to TNA to assume booking and in ring roles there too. He was finally brought into the WWE fold, where he stayed to the end of his life, signing a Legends contract and serving as a creative consultant. It makes perfect sense that Cody stands here now, ready to assume his backstage and in ring roles with AEW.

World Class Championship Wrestling, owned by Von Erich patriarch Fritz Von Erich, never booked Kerry and Kevin Von Erich in a feud with each other. Terry and Dory Jr. never played out a Funk brothers rivalry. It's a shame. We know and have seen the kind of heat that can draw. Look no further than Bret and Owen Hart's heated mid-90s rivalry. AEW has taken the natural road here, booking the older brother as the jealous one (as opposed to jealous younger Owen in the WWE) against the king of the company brother.

In a way, they're both fighting to establish a longer Rhodes legacy, one free of WWE's influence. While WWE has been kind to the Rhodes of late, this was not always the case. In the 1980s Vince McMahon did his fair share to rib and bury the American Dream. Dusty made a huge name for himself before he ever wrestled for the WWF. And if you've paid attention to WWF/E's history, it isn't always kind to the guys that were big time outside of its confines. Harley Race, *an NWA legend, was booked as an afterthought during his WWF run with hardly any mention of his prominence in other promotions. Vince went even further though to diminish Dusty's persona.*

Before Dusty ever signed with the WWF, Vince had his eyes on mocking The American Dream. He took the proven One Man Gang gimmick off of George Gray and put the "Akeem the African Dream" outfit on him. Gray was forced to constantly "jive," a head and hand bob that Vince invented to parody the moving and shaking of Dusty. Dusty's east Texas accent was confused as an affected black soul jive lingo by the WWF, so Akeem was the "African Dream," or a white man pretending to be black. When Ted DiBiase was assigned a black manservant, he was dubbed "Virgil," a direct reference to Dusty Rhodes' real name, Virgil Runnels.

When the WWF did finally lure Dusty, because he was unhappy with WCW management at the time, Vince put Dusty in polka dots and into storyline with the completely talentless Sapphire (Juanita Wright was a superfan and regional promotion referee, but her mic and in ring skills were complete crap in the WWF). Vince couldn't wait to put Dusty into storyline as a mixed-race couple because he couldn't let go his perception that Dusty was imitating black men. Until very, very recently the WWE treated Dusty Rhodes with very little reverence indeed.

AEW appears to offer a new chance for the Rhodes legacy to leave a giant mark in the annals of wrestling lore, one free of

*Turner or McMahon promotional whims, one that is instead
Rhodes-centred.*

*AEW's calling card might be their resistance to the WWE
route, but frankly I'm glad they've extended the sibling
rivalry featured and developed over a few year period in
WWE as Goldust and Cody, then Stardust, teamed then
feuded. For the most part, AEW has molded itself as the
anti-WWE. Cody put Triple H and Goldust and the
Attitude Era on blast for a reason. They paved the way for
the popularity of wrestling, but Cody and Kenny Omega and
others stand ready to showcase what WWE has often
avoided: putting the best in-ring performers, not the best
bodies or most constructed characters, over. That said, it's a
good thing they haven't ignored the past completely in
paving the way forward for the Rhodes family and AEW
wrestling.*

Dustin versus Cody should be something to see indeed.

REMEMBERING RIC FLAIR VS. KERRY VON ERICH 35 YEARS LATER

By
Paul
Posted on May 7, 2019

THE NIGHT I WAS BORN, RIC FLAIR DEFEATED HARLEY RACE IN A STEEL CAGE AT THE FIRST EVER STARRCADE TO WIN THE NWA WORLD TITLE IN FRONT OF NEARLY 16,000 FANS IN GREENSBORO, NORTH CAROLINA.

That same night, Fritz Von Erich's Dallas-based promotion, World Class Championship Wrestling, held the Thanksgiving Star Wars featuring three of the former wrestler turned promoter sons, David Von Erich, Kerry Von Erich, and Mike Von Erich, the latter in his debut match, in front of over 19,000 attendees at Dallas' Reunion Arena.

November 24, 1983 was indeed a banner night in the history of wrestling.

That night set up a collision course for another red letter day for wrestling, the biggest match in wrestling history before Hogan slammed Andre at the Pontiac Silverdome at Wrestlemania III; 35 years ago Kerry Von Erich beat Ric Flair for that same NWA World Title in front of over 50,000 fans at Texas Stadium, May 6, 1984.

Thing is, it was never really meant to be that way. It wasn't Kerry's shot. He was there on a coin toss because David Von Erich, the brother groomed to hold the NWA belt, died after the Thanksgiving Star Wars, February 10, 1984, in a hotel room in Japan. The official cause of death was listed ruptured intestines, supported by Fritz and his other sons saying David had suffered a brutal blow to the sternum in a match in Japan the day before. History has proven this claim false though as David never made it into the ring on that tour.

Many wrestlers have told and written a different version of events with a straight face, including Ric Flair himself. Flair and others relate that the second man in the room, Bruiser Brody, a star for WCCW and fierce friend of the Von Erich family, disposed of the empty painkiller bottle that remained after David overdosed.
This version really does seem a more true turn of events when it comes to the Von Erich boys. David categorically did not wrestle in Japan so the Von Erich version definitely isn't true. When you look at the fact that Mike Von Erich died of intentional overdose of alcohol and sleeping pills. According to interviews with Kevin Von Erich, the only surviving Von Erich, Mike left youngest brother Chris the same pills for when he felt the time to bow out. Chris eschewed this and shot himself in 1991. The man who wrestled in the biggest match on the planet at the time, Kerry, would shoot himself nine years after beating Flair at Texas Stadium with a backslide for the World Title. Suicide

runs in the Von Erich family—it makes it easy to believe Flair's version of events around David's death are closer to the truth.

Flair was at the center of the Von Erich wrestling world in late 1983 through May of 1984. And his main rival during this time was David, not Kerry. David beat Flair for the NWA Missouri Heavyweight title September 16, 1983. He transitioned the belt to Missouri legend Harley Race in January of 1984 after Flair took the World Title off Race at Starrcade. At the time of the 1983 Thanksgiving Star Wars David was Texas Heavyweight Champion (he retained his title against Kamala that night). On Christmas night, December 25, 1983, Flair and David Von Erich battled for the World Title in Dallas with Flair retaining the belt.

After beating David on Christmas, Flair cut a promo on Mike's inability to wrestle (not far from he truth as the younger boys Mike and Chris was never considered as good of in-ring workers as older boys Kevin, David, and Kerry). This lead to a special challenge from David: if Mike could last in a cage for ten minutes with Flair without being pinned, Flair would have to put his title up against David again under any stipulations David wanted. Mike did last ten minutes on January 30, 1984 and David had his shot. In truth, the NWA voting committee had decided in January of 1984 to put the NWA World Title on David Von Erich some time in March or April of 1984.

Fritz Von Erich had been a legendary heel in his time, but due to his Nazi persona and his temperamental relationship with several promoters throughout his career, he was perhaps the most legendary non-NWA World Champion ever. His chase for the better turned into the Von Erich quest for the belt once Fritz was retired and his sons wrestled for his promotion.

The delay was needed because Fritz had already booked David to tour Japan. Every the economic opportunist, Fritz was one of the first wrestling promoters to see international tours and international talent exchanges as a way to increase his profits. This along with his contract with the international broadcasting contracts WCCW had with the Christian Broadcasting Network and ESPN made Von Erich's Dallas based promotion arguably the most popular in the world pre-WrestleMania. Even when David, according to Kevin, complained of illness before his flight to Japan, Fritz was insistent David take the flight and the tour.

David never came back. The match with Flair to take place sometime after the return in March or April 1984 would not come to be.

Fritz talked to every microphone that would listen about the death of David as a freak accident of the ring, and that the best way to honor David's legacy was for one of the other Von Erich boys, Kerry or Kevin, to carry on the quest and win the NWA Title. Listen to the Lapsed Fan Wrestling Podcast's recent multi-week Von Erich episodes or the recent

VICELAND'S Dark Side of the Ring episode on the Von Erichs, and you'll start to cringe at how much Fritz deflected the emotional impact of one tragedy in his family after another and continuously hucked the Von Erich name and his WCCW wrestling promotion on the back of such tragedies.

Whatever the motivations, Fritz's lobbying worked and it was agreed that at a special David Von Erich Memorial Parade of Champions at Texas Stadium on May 6, 1984 that Ric Flair would drop the NWA World Title to a Von Erich brother. But which one? According to again the only surviving source of Von Erich lore, oldest brother Kevin, there was a simple coin toss to see if bare-foot high flyer Kevin would face Flair, or the muscled-up heartthrob Kerry would be the one. Kerry won the coin toss.

There was a reason that David, not older Kevin nor younger but bigger Kerry was booked for the NWA title. Though all the brothers struggled with drug addictions, Kerry struggled the most and hid it the least. Flair writes in his autobiography of several Kerry matches where Kerry was so smacked out of his head he did things like wrestle without tying his boots, forget intricately worked-out match sequences, and leave in the middle of the match to hit on women in the crowd. That was of course if he didn't no-show an event, for which he became notorious. Kevin never struggled as publicly with his addictions, but unlike David or Kerry, he had little flair on the mic. David, was the best amalgamation of the three qualities needed to carry the NWA belt territory to territory: he wrestled well in the ring, could cut a promo, and could uphold the schedule of a champion without succumbing to drink or drugs too easily (he was after all the one sent to Japan to represent WCCW).

Plans, of course, changed after David died. What might have been a long Von Erich reign atop the NWA became really only a moment.

But that moment was huge. Over 50,000 fans packed Texas Stadium on May 6, 1984. Besides the central bout, Flair versus Kerry for the title, Fritz had come out of retirement for one match only, to team with sons Kevin and Mike against the Fabulous Freebirds.

When he came to the ring, Kerry wore a sequined jacket with his brother's name on the back along with a yellow rose (David had been nicknamed the "Yellow Rose of Texas" after the well-known folk song). The crowd erupted for the hometown hero.

The match is mostly vintage Flair. He takes a toss from the top rope. He chops. He flops. He goes for the Figure Four, but Kerry blocked Flair's finisher, then reversed a Flair hip toss into a backslide that won the title. The crowd goes absolutely ape. The pop is as loud as, if not louder than, the Silverdome when Hogan slammed Andre three years later.

Kerry's family, including his mother Doris, come out to celebrate and honor David.

The celebration was short-lived, however. Kerry was already notorious for blowing off matches, wrestling intoxicated, and no-showing events. The NWA committee was not going to let Von Erich hold on to the belt very long. Attuned to the emotional nature of the situation given David's death, the NWA was smart enough to book Kerry losing the belt back to Flair just eighteen days later in Japan. Flair held the belt for another two years before losing it to the American Dream Dusty Rhodes in July of 1986.

After this, the Von Erichs descended into further tragedy. Ever eager to keep his Texas wrestling empire in the green, Fritz eschewed overtures from Vince McMahon and urged his sons to do the same. Kerry did eventually go to the WWF as the Texas Tornado where most remember him as an Ultimate Warrior seem-alike and his Intercontinental Title win over Mr. Perfect (though again, Vince did not trust Kerry to carry the belt through many events and took the belt off Kerry within 3 months in a day when IC champs tended to reign for the better part of a year or more). Little did many know at the time, but Kerry made this run without a foot, as he had a bad motorcycle accident and had returned too soon to the ring, at his father's urging, reinjuring the foot, necessitating amputation. Shortly after his WWF run, in 1993, Kerry was busted for control substance (again), and shot and killed himself at just 33 years old.

He lived less time than it has been since that historic day in May 1984.

Flair, of course, went on to be the workhorse champ of the NWA, then WCW when Jim Crockett's NWA promotion was bought and renamed by media mogul Ted Turner. Flair played a major part at some point in every major promotion save ECW since the 1990s.

What should have been the world's introduction to the Von Erichs in May 1984 and kickstarted international cross-promotions really became the single pinnacle, the heights they would not reach again. Because of Kerry's inability to stay clean, Kevin's unwillingness to take the spotlight (he turned down WWF and WCW contracts several times), and Fritz's refusal to work with any promotion save his own Dallas-based one, the Von Erich family story simply became tragedy after tragedy. After David died Mike died, then Chris died, then Kerry died, then Fritz died.

Sad but true, what we are left with is to simply say that 35 years ago, on the back of tragedy, Kerry Von Erich did win the world title in the biggest wrestling match ever at the time.

Acknowledgments

Thanks much to Gimmick Press and TWM News for letting me hone some of this and my wrestling writing chops with previous publication of a few pieces herein. Thanks much to Sheldon Lee Compton, Benjamin Drevlow, Jared Yates Sexton, Mike T. Chin, Gonzalo Baeza, Josh Olsen, Joey R. Poole, Vernon Smith, Bill Soldan, and Frank Reardon — a writing tribe I'm mighty mighty grateful for. This book is very much born of the dangerous feeling of nostalgia — still, I'd be remiss not to acknowledge the stars of 80s and 90s wrestling on television for breeding that nostalgia, the OSW Review and the Lapsed Fan boys for indulging that nostalgia, and my wife for putting up with that nostalgia.

Made in the USA
Middletown, DE
20 September 2019